CHRISTMAS WITCH LIST

A WESTWICK WITCHES COZY MYSTERY

COLLEEN CROSS

SLICE MYSTERY AND THRILLER BOOKS

Christmas Witch List

Copyright © 2018 by Colleen Cross, Colleen Tompkins

All rights reserved. No part of this publication may be reproduced, stored in a retrieval system, or transmitted in any form or by any means—electronic, mechanical, recording, or otherwise—without the prior written consent of the copyright holder and publisher. The scanning, uploading and distribution of this book via the Internet or any other means without the permission of the publisher is illegal and punishable by law.

Please purchase only authorized electronic editions, and do not participate in or encourage electronic piracy of copyrighted materials. Your support of the author's rights is appreciated.

This is a work of fiction. Names, characters, places, and incidents either are the product of the author's imagination or are used fictitiously, and any resemblance to actual persons, living or dead, business establishments, events, or locales is entirely coincidental.

Categories: cozy mysteries, witches wizards, paranormal cozy humorous mystery, cosy mystery, funny mysteries, female lead sleuth women amateur sleuths private investigators, cozy mystery books, suspense thrillers and mysteries best sellers, female detectives

eBook ISBN: 978-1-988272-16-0

Published by Slice Publishing

CHRISTMAS WITCH LIST

Cendrine West is looking forward to a cozy Christmas Eve dinner when a blizzard blows in, bringing with it a flurry of unexpected guests. But tipsy witches and mischievous magic spell a recipe for disaster, especially when a guest turns up dead. Cen's sleuthing exposes a Santa-sized sack of trouble and everyone's a suspect, even her hunky sheriff boyfriend.

Is it a deadly accident by a drunken witch…or something more sinister? Murder is on the menu and only magic can uncover the truth in this witchy, wacky Yuletide thrill ride!

Witch cozy mysteries are for fans of fun, cozy mystery books with a paranormal twist! If you haven't already read the first 3 books in the series, *Witch You Well*, *Rags to Witches*, and *Witch and Famous*, get them now in a specially priced Westwick Witches Magical Mystery box set.

"Five stars for my favorite combo of magic, mistletoe, and murder!"

"...A bewitching, supernatural treat. If you love witch cozy mysteries you'll love Cendrine West and her wacky witch family!"

"...One of the best paranormal mystery books I've read in awhile. An imaginative detective mystery that combines the best mysteries of an Agatha Christie whodunit novel with a Harry Potter fantasy book, this is magic for grown-ups!"

Sign up for Colleen's new release notifications at http://eepurl.com/bkYx01 or visit http://www.colleencross.com

It's Christmas Eve with freshly fallen snow,
Witches kiss loved ones under mistletoe,
The Wests are hosting some unusual guests,
At least one of whom is on a romantic quest.

The witches are up to old tricks again,
Always looking for witch rules to bend,
Until something makes their stomachs churn,
That's when things take a surprising turn.

The witches imbibe too much food and drink,
Soon it is clear they are all on the brink,
Of magic and mayhem out of control,
That threatens to send them to the North Pole.

Despite all of the holiday good cheer,
One of their guests will pay very dear.
Meanwhile, a blizzard blows outside,
Buckle up for a thrilling Yuletide ride!

CHAPTER 1

Christmas is my favorite time of year. This year was extra special because it was my first holiday with Tyler. Just the thought of my tall, hunky boyfriend brought a smile to my lips. I couldn't wait to see him. He was still at work and running a bit late because of the massive snowstorm that had enveloped Westwick Corners and cut us off from the rest of the world.

His delayed arrival just made my anticipation sweeter. My pulse quickened as I imagined kissing him, his strong arms wrapped around my waist. Our first Christmas Eve would be a holiday we would both remember and cherish for a long, long time.

As Westwick Corners sheriff and only law enforcement, Tyler Gates was always busy. Mostly because of Aunt Pearl, who repeatedly broke the law and generally made life rough for Tyler. Her number one priority was to drive him out of town as she had done to all of the sheriffs before him.

I had expected tonight to be different, partly because Aunt Pearl wasn't out stirring up trouble for him in the snowstorm. Instead, she had hung out around the house all day with the rest of my family. That was unusual for my anti-social aunt. But the strangest thing of all was that it was Aunt Pearl who had invited Tyler to join us for our traditional family Christmas Eve dinner in the first place.

I had planned our holiday festivities for weeks, down to the tiniest detail. Christmas was the only time of year where we closed our family business and took a break from our busy lives.

Being a witch doesn't come with a paycheck, so we all needed jobs to make ends meet. We had converted our family mansion into the Westwick Corners Inn, a cozy boutique bed and breakfast. Also on our property was a small estate winery and the Witching Post Bar and Grill, a pub that catered mostly to locals.

Our family home had been repurposed out of necessity because there weren't any viable jobs in our almost-ghost town. All that changed for one short week at Christmastime when we closed and repurposed the inn as our family gathering place once more.

Aside from my duties at the inn, I also ran a newspaper, the West-wick Corners Weekly. I had just published the Christmas edition and even had my articles written for the following week. Nothing much ever happened in tiny Westwick Corners, so I could afford to shut down my one-woman newspaper operation over the holidays.

I had looked forward to Christmas Eve dinner for weeks and wanted it to be the start of many holidays to remember with Tyler.

Yet it wasn't working out that way at all.

I had the white Christmas I had been dreaming of, but the winter wonderland outside had morphed into a snowy prison. There were already several feet of snow on the ground and more fell by the hour. All that would be perfect if Tyler and I were snuggled in front of a roaring fire while snowflakes blanketed the grounds outside.

Instead, Tyler was stuck out on the highway helping stranded motorists. I shut my eyes and sighed. If only the storm had held off for one more day. I shivered at the thought of Tyler possibly being stranded. The roads were treacherous. It was already dark outside, and I hadn't heard from him all day. I worried that he wouldn't make it in time for Christmas Eve dinner.

Normally I loved the muffled quiet that came with a thick blanket of snow, but tonight was different. The winter storm had blown in quickly and unexpectedly this morning with strong winds and snow-drifts high enough to bury cars. If anything the snow fell harder now. I closed my eyes and imagined Tyler and me finally together and standing under the mistletoe. Now my anticipation was tinged with worry.

I pulled my cell phone from my pocket and called him. It seemed like forever before he answered.

"Cen…I meant to call you." Tyler's deep voice sounded distant and staticky. "I just finished dealing with a stalled semi-trailer. The road's almost impassable now, but I'm on my way. I'll be there soon. Miss you."

"I miss you too." Just imagining Tyler's warm brown eyes made me smile. We saw each other daily. In fact, it was hard not to constantly run into each other in our tiny little almost-ghost town. Lately though, we had both been working long hours so that we could enjoy some uninterrupted time off together. "I'll tell Mom to hold off dinner, just get here as fast as you can."

I sighed as I disconnected. Then I remembered the other wrench in my plans.

Merlinda.

Aunt Pearl's star student hadn't gone home to Vanuatu for the holidays as planned. The flight back to her South Pacific tropical paradise had been canceled due to the snowstorm. Now, she was spending Christmas with us.

Merlinda was an extremely powerful witch-in-training. Every-thing came to her effortlessly. Basically, she was everything that I wasn't. It wasn't that I didn't like her. In fact, I barely knew her at all. She was always immersed in a spell book and mostly kept to herself. I only saw her in passing because she boarded at our family's inn while Pearl's Charm School was in session.

Now Merlinda was part of our special family time and I didn't like it one bit. I almost felt like a stranger in my own home with her here. Aunt Pearl doted on her pet student and basically ignored the rest of us. Even Mom and Aunt Amber seemed completely charmed by Merlinda. Next to her, I felt incompetent as a witch. I also felt invisible.

Merlinda's spellcasting rivaled the best in the business, and she wasn't even finished with school yet. She was gorgeous too. Her dark exotic looks turned heads on the few occasions when she ventured into town. She never socialized, but that made her all the more alluring and mysterious to just about every male in Westwick Corners. They were captivated by both her beauty and her charming South Pacific accent.

I should have been helping Mom and Aunt Amber in the kitchen with dinner but steered clear because they were sure to notice my sour mood. Instead, I glanced around the living room, hoping that the festive decor would lift my spirits.

For witches, we were pretty traditional when it came to Christmas Eve. The living room was fully decorated with lights, decorations, and tinsel for the season. A seven-foot Christmas tree stood on one side of the fireplace, and Mom's handcrafted Christmas stockings hung from the mantle. There was a hand-beaded felt stocking for each of us: Mom, Aunt Amber, Aunt Pearl, and me. And one extra that Mom had sewn for Merlinda this morning after Merlinda found out about her canceled flight home.

Having Merlinda here just ruined everything. I felt guilty thinking that way, but I also had a feeling that her presence would bring out a lot of bad in Aunt Pearl. And, I had to admit, I was more than a little jealous of Merlinda. Witchcraft and everything else just came to her so effortlessly.

As if on cue Merlinda and Aunt Pearl burst through the front door, laughing as they kicked off their snow-covered boots in the hallway.

That was the other thing that annoyed me. My cranky, fire-setting aunt was normally a loner and a troublemaker, keen on stirring up trouble and driving sheriffs like Tyler out of town. Yet in Merlinda's presence, she had morphed into a giggling do-gooder intent on spreading white magic far and wide. With Merlinda, of course, not with me.

Aunt Pearl and Merlinda spilled out into the living room, seeming not to notice me as they laughed about an advanced spell that was far beyond my abilities. Heck, I couldn't even understand what they were talking about. Within minutes they were spellcasting holograms of elves and reindeer, trying to outdo each other.

Aunt Pearl had even dressed for dinner. She wore a green velvet pantsuit, probably chosen for practical reasons. It looked festive and dressy while still allowing unrestricted movement for her so-called athletic pursuits. What she called athletic pursuits I considered arson, as did most of the people in town who kept up a fire watch, or rather a Pearl watch, during better weather. Hopefully Christmas Eve dinner and the storm outside provided enough distraction to keep her out of trouble for one night.

Tyler, as Westwick Corners' only law enforcement, was already run off his feet with today's snow-related events. He didn't need to spend Christmas Eve on an Aunt Pearl crime watch. That is, once he finally made it here.

My thoughts were interrupted by the jingle of Aunt Pearl's charm bracelet as she waved her arm with a flourish.

Merlinda laughed, exposing a brilliant white smile.

Any jealousy I felt was solely my fault. Merlinda couldn't help being beautiful. And I had only myself to blame for not studying my craft more. No wonder Aunt Pearl was so frustrated with me.

Witchcraft was practically the West family business. It didn't pay all that well, though. In fact, it didn't pay at all. That was the reason we each had jobs running the inn. Paying guests brought in much-needed cash. Operating an inn wasn't quite as glamorous as witchcraft, but at least it paid the bills.

"Too bad Earl couldn't make it." It was vindictive of me, but I couldn't help myself. Merlinda couldn't stand Earl. He was either Aunt Pearl's most ardent admirer or her secret boyfriend, depending on who you talked to. He was also competition for Merlinda.

Earl was a sweet, harmless seventyish local, a retired farmer and widower who had recently sold his farm to move into town. I had no idea what an easygoing man like Earl saw in Aunt Pearl or why Merlinda despised him so much. They both constantly vied for Aunt Pearl's attention. Merlinda's jealousy of Earl was the only crack I saw in her otherwise perfect demeanor.

"Earl's not coming," Aunt Pearl snapped. "The storm's too much for him."

"What a shame." That only reminded me that Tyler was still out in the elements dealing with the snowstorm. As the weather outside worsened, so did my hopes of a romantic, intimate Christmas.

Aunt Pearl scowled. "Cen, pay attention! You might learn something. You'd be a better witch by now if you focused like Merlinda does."

Merlinda whispered something in a low voice as she swept her long black hair over her shoulder.

The light in the room brightened like a sunny day. As it did, the sound of lapping water turned into crashing waves. A three-foot crystal glass ball floated several inches above Merlinda's outstretched hands, pulsating with energy and light. Inside was a kaleidoscopic view of a tropical island complete with palm trees, cabanas, and a swim-up bar.

A ukulele strummed softly.

A tropical paradise under glass, complete with a theme song.

How could I compete with that?

Merlinda was at least as good a witch as Aunt Pearl. Or maybe even better. I had never even considered that possible because until now, Aunt Pearl was the most powerful witch I had ever seen.

Not anymore.

Needless to say, Merlinda's abilities were beyond the realm of my talents by a long shot. I couldn't even conjure up a glass of water if my life depended on it, let alone create a seaside paradise in the palm of my hand. I fake-smiled, hoping that the resentment burning inside me didn't show.

"Bravo!" Aunt Amber clapped as she stood in the dining room doorway, an amazed expression on her face. "That's the best version of that spell I've ever seen."

No wonder Aunt Pearl adored Merlinda.

She was the perfect student and protégé. Nice to a fault, eager to learn, and from what I could see, she pretty much exceled at everything. Merlinda didn't stand up to Aunt Pearl's tantrums or ever question her pyromaniac pranks either. In Aunt Pearl's eyes, she was perfect.

No wonder Merlinda was the teacher's pet. I couldn't blame Aunt Pearl. I, on the other hand, was a Pearl's Charm School dropout. I never really cared about my spellcasting prowess before because sorcery wasn't my chosen career path.

Yet the path was chosen for me nonetheless. Even if I chose not to use witchcraft on a daily basis it still remained part of my identity as a witch. Aunt Pearl says it's my destiny whether I like it or not. It's my duty to cast spells, cook up potions and perform other witchy duties as required. It's that last item in the job description that nags at me. Why can't I just exercise my own free will and live an ordinary life?

Because no matter how hard I try, I just don't seem to possess the family talents. Mom excels at herbal potions and magical amulets while Aunt Amber is an expert spellcaster. Aunt Pearl is an all-around master of all witchcraft disciplines, so she gravitates to teaching. She expects to turn out expert witches at Pearl's Charm School. Anything less is unacceptable.

I, on the other hand, have mastered none of those things. Partly because I'm risk-averse (definitely *not* ideal in a witch) and partly because I lack discipline. I'm better at fact-finding, logic, and journalistic endeavors; something Aunt Pearl calls my failed backup plan. She never lets me live it down.

"See how it's done, Cendrine?" Aunt Pearl only used my full name when she was either mad or annoyed with me. She clasped her hands together as she nodded toward her star student. "You can't expect success unless you put in the work. Right, Merlinda?"

Merlinda flushed at the mention of her name. Or maybe she was embarrassed by Aunt Pearl's criticism of me.

"That's my house next to the coral reef." Merlinda pointed to a palatial estate on a cliff that jutted above a turquoise blue sea. "I love Westwick Corners, but I really wanted to be back home for the holidays. Seeing Vanuatu under glass is the next best thing to being there, I guess."

Waves lapped against the glass of the tropical snow globe as if in agreement.

"Wow, such detail. Your globe is beautiful." Aunt Amber, eggnog in hand, inched closer to Merlinda's tropical snow globe to get a better look. "Hey, is that your island?"

Merlinda nodded. "It is. Vanuatu in real time."

"That's amazing." Aunt Amber grimaced as she swallowed a mouthful of eggnog. "Something about this eggnog is a bit off. I must have added too much nutmeg."

We all stared at the globe, mesmerized by the tiny people who moved around the large beachfront estate. Miniature cars drove by on the nearby road. A gray-haired couple sat hand-in-hand on the large terrace while several men tended the large formal gardens that surrounded the mansion. It reminded me of a museum diorama except that everyone was moving. It was a reality show where the stars had no idea they were being watched.

Creepy when you thought about it.

"I can almost feel the tropical breeze. Much better than Google Earth." Aunt Amber tucked a lock of red hair behind her ear as she gazed at the crystal globe. "You sure are talented, Merlinda."

"I was just lucky with the spell this time." Merlinda shrugged.

"How come it's daylight inside the globe? It's already dark outside." I was secretly pleased to point out her mistake.

"That's because it's already tomorrow there," Merlinda said. "Vanuatu is about a thousand miles east of Australia."

"Oh." I wished I had kept my mouth shut. I felt dumb for not realizing the time zone difference.

"Which makes your Vanuatu globe even more amazing. It's your supernatural skills, not luck." Aunt Pearl beamed at Merlinda. Then she turned to me, a mischievous glint in her eye. "Cendrine, why don't you give it a try?"

Aunt Pearl knew very well that I wasn't capable of anything close to that. It was a trap to embarrass me so I changed the subject. "Who are those people?"

"Those are my parents on the terrace," Merlinda said. "The rest are the household staff."

"Try it yourself, Cendrine." Aunt Pearl fake-smiled at me. "Practice for the games."

Christmas Eve witchcraft games were a West family tradition, but I was mostly an observer. I had done a few spells of my own, but only in the presence of my family. I wasn't about to spell cast in front of Merlinda. Aside from the intense pressure to perform, I was certain that Aunt Pearl's request came with strings attached.

"I'd rather not. Let's just have a normal Christmas Eve," I protested. "Without witchcraft."

"But we always do spells," Aunt Amber protested. "Christmas Eve without spellcraft is like chocolate cake without icing. How else will we pass the time?"

"Other families manage just fine." I scanned the room for Mom to rescue me, but she was still busy in the kitchen.

"Well, we aren't exactly a typical family now, are we?" Aunt Amber drained the rest of her eggnog and placed her empty glass on the coffee table. "C'mon Cen, give it a shot."

I shook my head. "You both promised that we would act normal tonight."

"Normal?" Aunt Pearl asked. "You mean as in a non-witch family? Honestly, Cendrine, you are so ungrateful. You take your witch talents totally for granted. You just don't know how lucky you are."

She shook her head slowly. "Tonight is just like any other West family Christmas Eve. Merlinda is practically family. She has generously shared a snapshot of a Vanuatu Christmas with us. Why can't you share something too?"

Now she had really put me on the spot. Aunt Pearl was definitely up to something, but what? "Merlinda's already done a great job. What could I possibly add?"

Aunt Pearl scratched her chin. "You could show Merlinda what a real Westwick Corners Christmas is like."

I shrugged. "It's exactly like this."

"You know what I mean," Aunt Pearl said. "With all the bells and whistles."

I didn't know but got the sense that she was about to show me. I glanced at Merlinda. She remained fixated on Aunt Pearl, adoration in her eyes.

Their mutual love fest was super annoying.

"Wow, Vanuatu sure is beautiful. Maybe we should plan a family vacation there," Aunt Amber said. "You must be so disappointed to have missed your flight home."

Merlinda gazed wistfully outside at the large snowflakes that dropped like invading paratroopers. "It's okay. Now I get to experience a white Christmas. It never snows in Vanuatu, so it never really felt like Christmas."

She flicked her wrist and the globe floated toward the Christmas tree. It hovered briefly before nestling into the branches about halfway up the tree.

I scanned the living room. Mini snowdrifts adorned the square windowpanes and framed the winter wonderland outside. Our majestic Christmas tree was laden with decorations and crowned with a twinkling star.

And now it was also adorned with Merlinda's magical crystal globe. Her Christmas takeover was complete.

The yuletide scene was straight out of a Hallmark card. But in the West family emotions always simmered just below the surface, in particular between Aunt Pearl and Aunt Amber. Our dinners usually devolved to bickering before dessert, but with Merlinda here maybe they would put aside their sibling rivalry. They seemed to be making an effort for the moment at least.

I refocused on Merlinda. For the first time, I felt a little sorry for her, away from her own family at this time of year. "I know it's nothing like what you're used to, but Westwick Corners is quite nice at Christmas, even with a snowstorm."

"We can make it even better," Aunt Pearl said. "We'll recreate Cen's childhood Christmas so you can experience it first-hand!"

"What a great idea," Aunt Amber said. "Total immersion. Bring it on!"

I opened my mouth to speak but nothing came out. Instead, a shock of frigid air invaded my lungs and took my breath away. I coughed so hard I fell backward. I pushed myself back up into a sitting position only to find myself no longer in the living room. What I had mistaken for the overstuffed armchair was actually powdery snow. In fact, I was up to my neck in it. Somehow, I was outside in sub-zero weather half-buried in a snowdrift.

Alone.

I shivered and rubbed my already-numb arms.

If Merlinda was supposed to be experiencing my Christmas, she was strangely absent. In fact, everyone was. Maybe the spell had gone wrong. Or maybe everyone was busy re-living my childhood Christmas except for me.

The low clouds made everything feel close and eerie. There were no recognizable buildings or landmarks that I could see. Just snow-drifts everywhere.

Something else was amiss. It was still daylight. Either it was a few hours earlier in the afternoon, which would have involved a tricky time travel spell, or I was trapped inside a time-delayed winter snow globe. I guessed the latter, because I knew Mom would have a fit if Aunt Pearl had sent me back in time on Christmas Eve.

But if the others were outside the globe, I couldn't see or hear them. I thought I felt their presence, but maybe that was just wishful thinking. I felt like a zoo animal, on display under glass in someone else's show. Except the snow was very real. It swirled down around me, the wet flakes coating my bare arms. I shivered and wondered if this was another of Aunt Pearl's tricks designed to keep Tyler and me apart.

What if he arrived only to find me gone? All kinds of scenarios flashed through my mind. What if Aunt Pearl sent him out in the storm to search for me?

My heart sank with the realization that Aunt Pearl was up to her old tricks again, thwarting any chance of a cozy, romantic yuletide. She despised Tyler because whenever she broke the law, he fined her. He never let her get away with anything. Her grudge against him was now directed at me, in the hopes that I would stop dating him.

Well, I wasn't giving up that easily.

But for the moment, at least, I was trapped. Locked out of my world at the whim of ornery Aunt Pearl, who acted more like a terrible two-year-old than the seventy-two-year-old she actually was.

I crossed my arms and shivered from the cold. My sleeveless dress was hardly suited to the frigid temperatures and the worsening snowfall. Within minutes I would be hypothermic. Surely Aunt Pearl would rescue me before frostbite set in.

But in case she didn't, I needed a backup plan. I scanned my surroundings, noting an old-fashioned sleigh nearby that I hadn't noticed before. I approached it from the rear and noted that the sleigh resembled a horse-drawn carriage, only much larger. The open carriage was piled high with boxes of cargo. The boxes obscured my view and left nowhere to sit or stand.

I trudged through the thigh-deep snow and circled partway around the sleigh before a gust of wind almost knocked me over. I ducked underneath the rear of the carriage for shelter. Snow seeped into my ankle-length boots, and my bare legs grew so numb from the cold that I could barely feel them.

The wind howled and grew stronger. What little shelter the sleigh provided was offset by my skin contact with the snow. Now my butt was numb too. Staying here meant freezing to death. I crawled back out and trudged toward the front of the sleigh.

My hopes soared when I realized I wasn't alone. They just as quickly faded when I saw the backside of a large man seated in the front seat.

As I got closer, recognition set in.

Santa Claus.

Oh, dear.

No, reindeer.

Eight of them and me.

I laughed out loud at the fake reindeer. The oversized lawn ornaments were signature Aunt Pearl. But if this was Aunt Pearl's magic, then why was I slowly freezing to death? She was incredibly thoughtless sometimes, but she wasn't cruel.

She also would have rescued me by now, especially with Aunt Amber in the room. Something had gone terribly wrong. Were the two of them so bewitched by Merlinda that they had forgotten all about me?

I leaned against the sleigh and formulated a plan. At least the sleigh provided a little shelter from the wind. I ducked back under the sleigh again, but the gap between the carriage bottom and the growing snowdrift had narrowed to only about eight inches.

This wasn't going to work. I stood helplessly as I wondered what to do. The snow was falling so hard around me that I would be buried before long.

I had to get out of this mess.

"Help!" I was close to tears.

Nobody answered. I sighed in defeat. It was almost dinnertime on Christmas Eve, and instead of relaxing with a drink by the fire, I was freezing to death inside a conjured-up Christmas snow globe.

I had to move while I still had control of my half-frozen legs. I lurched forward like a drunk, yet I hadn't touched a drop of alcohol. Without my bearings, I had no idea which way to go, so I headed in the same direction the sleigh pointed.

The ground beneath me rumbled.

I jumped as something jingled behind me. I turned and froze.

The reindeer.

They came to life in a flash. They snorted and pawed at the snowy ground like racehorses at the starting gate. They strained at the harness, pulling the sleigh with them. I was about to be run over by eight rambunctious reindeer, and there was no one to help me.

I stumbled through the snow, frantically trying to escape the unruly herd. But every time I changed direction, the reindeer did too.

The ground shook even harder, and as I teetered to keep my balance, my elbow hit something.

Glass.

I pounded on it with all my might. "Let me out!"

CHAPTER 2

"See, Cen? That's how you do a proper transport spell." Aunt Pearl gazed adoringly at Merlinda, completely oblivious to my hypothermia and quite possibly, frostbite.

Merlinda beamed.

"I could have frozen to death." My memory of the snow globe breakout was hazy. All I remembered was stampeding reindeer and shattered glass. My almost-frostbitten skin was very real, though.

My fingers burned as I gripped my wineglass. I had poured myself a generous glass of merlot before seating myself in the oversized armchair by the fireplace. I gulped it down as I slowly defrosted by the roaring fire. I still had no idea how I had escaped my snow globe prison. Or, for that matter, got back inside the house.

"Some people learn better by doing. Like you, Cendrine." Aunt Pearl smiled sweetly at me.

Aunt Amber gave me a sympathetic look. "Pearl forgot the last sentence of the spell. I had to help her a little."

Aunt Pearl rolled her eyes. "Oh, don't be ridiculous, Amber. I never forget anything. I did it on purpose, to build suspense. All part of the experience."

I downed the rest of my wine and set the glass down on the side table. I rubbed my hands together in front of the roaring fire. My fingers were still whitish blue, and they hurt like hell. "I think I have frostbite. How could you just leave me outside like that? I could have died."

Aunt Pearl rolled her eyes. "Geesh, Cen! You're like a hothouse flower. It's high time I helped you toughen up a little."

"You forgot all about me, didn't you?" I didn't know which was more alarming: that Aunt Pearl had forgotten me or that she had forgotten a spell. Maybe her age was catching up with her because she seemed a little foggy. A senile witch was no laughing matter.

My thoughts were interrupted by the doorbell.

Tyler. My heart soared as I visualized all six-foot-something of my hunky boyfriend in his sheriff's uniform. Now that he was here, we could finally start our Christmas together. Aunt Pearl, Merlinda, none of that mattered anymore.

I glanced out the living room window as I raced to the door. It was pitch black outside, and the wind had strengthened to almost gale force. It rattled the ancient single-pane windows and whistled down the fireplace.

Somehow Tyler had made it despite the storm, and nothing else mattered.

"It's about time that no-good boyfriend of yours showed up. Let's eat." Aunt Pearl shooed Merlinda and Aunt Amber into the dining room.

* * *

I IMMEDIATELY REGRETTED OPENING the front door. My normally cautious nature had abandoned me, either from the holiday spirit or from the wine and other spirits I had mixed for myself after the wine. I was still traumatized from my snow globe rescue, and this latest development sent my pulse racing. I hadn't expected to see anyone but Tyler. Certainly not the stranger who faced me now.

Neck tattoos peeked out from under his leather jacket. His hair was cropped short in an uneven crew cut, and he looked as though he hadn't slept for days.

My heart thumped in my chest. Home invasions and robberies happened elsewhere, in big cities and highway junction towns. Not in a small hamlet crippled by a Christmas Eve blizzard. As if on cue, a huge gust of wind blew the front door wide open and sprayed the threshold with sloppy wet snowflakes.

"Sorry, we're closed for the holidays." I reached back and fumbled for the door handle, careful not to take my eyes off the hulk of a man inches away. We had no guest bookings, and our bed and breakfast clientele was almost exclusively couples looking for a romantic getaway. This guy was definitely traveling solo.

He shrugged and scratched his unshaven face. "Yeah, I know."

It was already dark and getting late on Christmas Eve in the midst of a snowstorm. All good reasons why this guy shouldn't be here. I had a general bad feeling about the burly stranger that faced me across the threshold. What I lacked in supernatural witch abilities was made up with plenty of good old-fashioned common sense.

My primal brain told me to slam the door. My logical brain over-ruled and willed me to calm down. "If you need directions back to the highway I can help—"

"Nope, I'm not lost. I'm supposed to be here. What I mean is…I'm not here for a room." He smiled, exposing a gold tooth. "On second thought, maybe I am."

"Sorry, no vacancies tonight." I started to close the door, but the thirty-something man was intent on keeping it open. He stepped forward and placed his boot on the threshold, blocking me from closing the door.

I recoiled as I assessed my options. He had to be at least 250 pounds. His muscled torso was obvious even under his heavy winter jacket, which I guessed was from prison workouts and not the YMCA. His neck tattoos and hard expression backed that up.

I was no match physically, but I was a witch. I had other powers to remove him, if necessary.

If only I could remember how to use them.

Too bad I was a failed witch who couldn't remember more than bits and pieces of a dozen or so everyday magic spells. Nothing useful to repel a home invasion.

"Mom? Aunt Amber? Somebody come to the door," I turned and yelled in the direction of the dining room. Surely a household of witches had my back.

Or maybe not. No one answered my call. They couldn't hear me above the peals of laughter and clinking of glasses. I turned back to my adversary.

He smiled his gold toothy grin. "Sounds like you're having a party."

"You'd better get going, or you'll never make it back to the highway with the way the snow's piling up." I kept my voice calm and pointed to his vehicle, a gleaming black Cadillac Escalade SUV parked haphazardly in the middle of the driveway.

Probably stolen.

He leaned into the doorway, so close that I smelled coffee on his breath. "Nah. I'm in the right place. I'm here to meet someone."

"Like I said, the inn is closed. There's no one here…" I involuntarily stepped back, repulsed by his closeness as he towered over me.

He frowned and stomped the snow off his boots, leaving crusts of snow imprinted with boot treads on the front porch. Whatever his criminal intentions, at least he had some semblance of manners. I pushed the image of yellow crime scene tape out of my mind as I looked hopefully toward the driveway. But there was still no sign of Tyler's Jeep coming up the hill.

Nothing.

My heart thudded in my chest.

Other than Tyler we weren't expecting any visitors, and people didn't just drop in for impromptu visits on Christmas Eve. Not even locals because the Witching Post Bar and Grill was closed for the holidays too. Anyone who had missed the 'closed' sign at the foot of our long, unploughed driveway would soon abandon any attempt to drive up it.

Our inn was also on the outskirts of town, miles from the main highway. Most people couldn't find Westwick Corners even when they were looking for it, let alone get here in the snow. I also knew everyone in town, and the few visitors expected had already arrived earlier today. None of them were this guy. A mistake wasn't likely.

My heart thumped.

It really was a home invasion.

I stepped behind the door and started to close it. What the hell had I been thinking? The festive season had made me let my guard down.

The man stepped forward. Now half his body was planted firmly between the door and the doorjamb. "Sorry I'm late. Traffic's horrible."

I pressed back, hoping to dislodge his foot. "I think you're at the wrong—"

He ignored me and kept repeating himself. "So glad I finally made it. The snow's really sticking now. I barely got my Escalade up the hill. They aren't so hot in the snow."

I stared past him to the Escalade. It was kind of nervy to just leave it in the middle of our unploughed driveway. He had managed to make it up the hill in a foot of snow yet couldn't be bothered to drive another twenty feet or so to the parking lot. I brushed away my annoyance. It hardly mattered since we weren't expecting anyone.

Except for Tyler, who was now an hour overdue. What if something bad had happened to him? Or worse, what if something was about to happen to us? At least Tyler would see the black Escalade as a possible warning that he was walking into an ambush.

As sheriff, Tyler could take care of himself. But even a cop wouldn't expect a home invasion on Christmas Eve.

Despite the cold, I was sweating. I wiped my forehead with the back of my hand and willed myself to regain my composure.

"Are you lost?" My pulse quickened. Since Westwick Corners was so off the beaten track, that had to be the explanation. "Take a right at the bottom of the hill, drive about five miles and then turn left at the junction. That will get you back on the highway."

He didn't move an inch.

And my backup posse was already drunk and out of earshot.

CHAPTER 3

"You gonna let me in?" The stranger's penetrating green eyes locked on mine. A grin slowly spread across his face, and he held out his hand. "Aah…you don't know who I am, do you? I'm Dominic, Merlinda's partner."

Partner seemed an odd choice of words for this roughneck, but maybe language was a little more formal where he came from. I was vaguely aware that Merlinda had a boyfriend back in Vanuatu, but Dominic's accent sounded more Texan than South Pacific. Then again, Merlinda rarely mentioned him, so I knew next to nothing.

"Merlinda's boyfriend?" I released my death grip on the doorknob and shook his hand. Yet another interloper was joining us on Christmas Eve. So much for my cozy family celebration. "She never mentioned you were coming."

"You sound kind of disappointed."

"No. It's just that, well…never mind." Now that I was no longer afraid for my life I could study Dominic a little more objectively. He was good-looking in a rough, bad boy sort of way. And the dusting of snow that coated his close-cropped dark blonde hair gave him a certain charm.

Dominic inched his hulky body forward until he completely blocked the doorway. "Merlinda has no idea I'm here. It's supposed to be a surprise. Pearl knows all about it, though. She's the one who invited me to dinner tonight."

My mouth dropped open. Not just because Dominic had flown all the way here on the flimsy basis of a dinner invitation, but because Aunt Pearl was the most anti-social person I knew. She hated visitors of any kind and went to great lengths to avoid people. It was a constant source of friction with guests at the inn. Why was she suddenly so hospitable? Something didn't add up.

Aunt Pearl's enchantment with Merlinda had completely altered her personality. It wasn't just that she had invited a stranger to dinner. She had invited Dominic on Christmas Eve. I wasn't sure what was more unusual, Aunt Pearl's invitation or her forgetting to mention it.

Even Rudolph, Donner, and Blitzen weren't roadworthy with the blizzard tonight. It also meant that Dominic wasn't just here for dinner. He would have to stay with us overnight or possibly even longer. The town's only snow plow wouldn't see any action until the snow stopped. That would be Christmas Day at the earliest.

But dealing with the fallout was Aunt Pearl's problem. She made safety impossible at the best of times, so this could be a lesson learned. As I opened the door and motioned Dominic inside, it struck me that Merlinda hadn't even planned on being in Westwick Corners for Christmas. She only happened to be here because her flight had been canceled. When exactly had Aunt Pearl invited Dominic?

Dominic ran a palm through his hair. "Pearl really never mentioned inviting me for dinner?"

I shook my head and stood back as he brushed past me inside. "I'm afraid not."

Dominic held his palms outward in apology. "I meant to grab some wine, but all the stores are closed."

I waved my hand in dismissal. "No need. We've got plenty to drink." Our well-stocked bar could always be replenished from the Witching Post Bar and Grill if needed. Food wasn't an issue either since Mom always made too much. Maybe that was why Aunt Pearl had neglected to tell Mom. Or maybe they had both just neglected to tell me.

At any rate, with enough food and alcohol I could get through this.

Puddles pooled on the hardwood floor as Dominic kicked off his boots.

A spell could easily restore everything back to normal, but I was annoyed by his thoughtlessness. He was sloppy and the polar opposite of perfect Merlinda, yet I didn't really like either one. Maybe I was the one with the problem. I was getting crankier by the minute.

I fake-smiled and took Dominic's coat and hung it on the hall coatrack before leading him into the living room. I called out. "Merlinda, you have a visitor."

Merlinda's eyes widened in shock when she emerged from the dining room. She stood in the doorway for a moment without saying anything. Then she tottered over to Dominic in her high heels and hugged him.

He bent over and kissed her on the cheek.

She broke from his embrace and frowned. "You're supposed to be in Vanuatu. How did you get here in the storm?"

Dominic shrugged. "I flew into Shady Creek this morning. I meant to surprise you earlier, but with the storm and all, I barely made it. I've been traveling for more than five hours trying to get here. The roads are a complete mess."

"But I was coming home for Christmas," Merlinda said. "You knew that."

Dominic shrugged. "I know, but I planned to arrive before your flight left. With the storm and all, I didn't think I would make it."

"Good thing my flight out was canceled or we would have missed each other." Merlinda looked even more refined and princess-like when contrasted with her tattooed boyfriend. They made such an odd couple, and Merlinda didn't seem all that thrilled to see him. Her happy, effervescent mood from moments ago had evaporated.

Dominic's account struck me as odd. I wouldn't forget Tyler's travel plans in the same situation. Instead, I would be counting the days until his return. Dominic didn't act like a lovesick boyfriend either. Something didn't add up, but my alcohol-infused brain wasn't quite up to the analysis right now.

I had no idea how long it took to fly from Vanuatu to Seattle and then onto Shady Creek, but it was a long haul flight, probably at least twelve hours. Add on the drive to Westwick Corners in winter, and the idea of a surprise visit seemed awfully strange.

My shoulders slumped as I visualized Tyler still caught outside in the messy weather. He could miss all of Christmas Eve dinner and our special West family holiday celebrations too. I had been looking forward to sharing it with him.

"Five hours of driving is a long time," said Merlinda. "Shady Creek is only an hour away."

Dominic nodded. "The highway was a total mess. I was lucky to get the last SUV at the rental agency."

I flashed back to the Escalade outside. It seemed more fancy than snow-worthy, and I'd never seen anything remotely like it at Budget or Enterprise, especially not in Shady Creek. I suspected Dominic was lying, but why? It was a minor detail, but it also implied there was more to his story.

Suddenly my night looked a lot more interesting, even with Tyler late. What did gorgeous Merlinda see in this tough guy? Other than being fit, he was kind of scruffy and average looking. Nothing wrong with that, but Merlinda could date any guy she wanted. Whatever did she want with this one?

CHAPTER 4

The aroma of roast turkey and seasonings wafted toward us as we headed into the dining room.

I paused at the dining room doorway and ushered Merlinda and Dominic ahead of me. I felt a pang of sympathy for Tyler, still stuck working outside in the cold. My stomach growled and reminded me that I hadn't eaten since breakfast.

"First things first." Dominic spotted the mistletoe as they passed under the archway. He wrapped his arms protectively around Merlinda. He pulled her close and kissed her.

"Ouch." Merlinda suddenly pulled back, a pained expression on her face. She leaned against the doorway and doubled over in pain.

"What's wrong, babe?" Dominic brushed away a lock of Merlinda's dark hair and tenderly tucked it behind her ear.

"Stomach cramps. Pearl gave me some of her special milk thistle tea, though. I think I'm feeling a little better now." Merlinda looked up into Dominic's eyes and kissed him.

Dominic and Merlinda blocked the dining room doorway, and I was stuck behind them as long as they remained under the mistletoe.

The contrast between gorgeous, model-thin Merlinda and rough-looking Dominic was startling.

Dominic's arrival had an upside since his presence could disrupt the odd dynamic between Merlinda and Aunt Pearl. Now Aunt Pearl had to compete with Dominic for Merlinda's attention.

Aunt Amber suddenly appeared on the dining room side of the doorway. She stood inches from the couple. Wrapped in their embrace, they were oblivious to her presence.

"How sweet." Aunt Amber floated a few feet off the floor behind the couple and reached above her head to adjust the mistletoe. She tore off a sprig of the mistletoe while Dominic and Merlinda kissed. A piece of the plant fell onto Dominic's head, but he appeared not to notice.

I wasn't sure if Aunt Amber's comment referred to the affectionate couple or if she meant it as a jab at Aunt Pearl, who never made tea for anyone.

"Aunt Amber, get down!" I was alarmed at her blatant use of witchcraft in front of strangers. Aunt Amber was a top executive at the Witches International Community Craft Association and should have known better. Normally, she was such a stickler for rules. Maybe it was the effects of holiday cheer, but her flagrant disregard of WICCA regulations was alarming.

"Don't talk to me like I'm a dog, Cendrine." Aunt Amber hissed. "Show your aunt some respect."

I shrugged. "I just wanted to protect our family secrets. And keep you out of trouble with WICCA."

Aunt Amber sighed and rolled her eyes. "I'm not in any trouble. And I can take care of myself just fine."

Everyone seemed a little testy and on edge tonight. Holidays did that to people.

I glanced at Merlinda and Dominic. Still wrapped in their own little world, despite being in the middle of our little spat, they remained oblivious to Aunt Amber's shenanigans.

"What's the big deal?" Aunt Amber's feet were firmly planted on terra firma once more, but she still looked annoyed.

"We have a guest, remember?" It was unlikely but still possible that Dominic was unaware that his girlfriend was a witch and that Pearl's Charm School wasn't some time warp finishing school. But even if he knew of Merlinda's witchy talents, he didn't know about ours. I wanted to keep it that way. At least, I hoped that Merlinda hadn't revealed our secret. At any rate, we certainly shouldn't reveal special talents to a stranger.

"Oh, lighten up, Cen. It's Christmas." Aunt Amber walked unsteadily beside me. She was on her fourth booze-laced eggnog by my count. A little holiday cheer and all the rules fell by the wayside.

Merlinda broke from Dominic's embrace and frowned at me. "What's going on?"

I cursed my own stupidity. Merlinda and Dominic hadn't noticed Aunt Amber's levitation, but they had certainly noticed our raised voices.

Before I could answer, Aunt Amber handed Merlinda the sprig of mistletoe. "You need this, hon. Mistletoe has protective qualities. You're safe as long as you carry it."

Dominic rolled his eyes. "You don't need a dead plant to protect you. Your Vanuatu stalker can't harm you here. Especially not with me to protect you."

Dominic's promise seemed pointless since Westwick Corners was pretty much deserted in December. I doubted that even a stalker would make an effort to find the place. Merlinda hardly needed protection. Still, it begged the question. "You have a stalker?"

"It's really nothing. Dominic is exaggerating." Merlinda turned back to Dominic and smiled. "You're right. I am safe here. Any threats are thousands of miles away."

"What kind of threats? What exactly do they want from you?" Merlinda's life seemed so picture-perfect, and I couldn't imagine anything troubling her. What could possibly be sinister in an island paradise like Vanuatu? I imagined a sleepy South Pacific island without a cloud in sight.

Merlinda shrugged. "It doesn't matter. Dominic will protect me." She broke from his embrace and smiled.

"Anybody wantin' to hurt my babe has to come through me first." Dominic gripped Merlinda's arm firmly and steered her into the dining room. He escorted her to the dining room table and held out her chair. Once she was seated, he sat down beside her.

Aunt Amber and I followed the couple into the dining room. Christmas dinner suddenly seemed a lot more interesting.

"I've been planning my surprise visit for weeks. Pearl knows all about it," Dominic said. "Almost didn't make it because of the snow, though. I've got a big surprise for you, babe."

Merlinda looked a little apprehensive though she managed a slight smile. "What kind of surprise?"

Dominic didn't answer. Instead, he slapped his palm on the table. "Now where's Pearl? I'm dying to meet Merlinda's mentor in the flesh."

I smiled at the thought of my law-breaking, trouble-making aunt as anyone's mentor. I also couldn't wait to see Aunt Pearl tear into Dominic. Aside from hating men, she would consider Dominic a threat, vying for her star—and only—student's attention. Which made her invitation to him even more puzzling.

"I think she's in the kitchen," I said. "While we're waiting, can I get you something to drink?"

"Got any beer?"

I headed into the kitchen where Mom and Aunt Pearl stood with their backs to me. Mom stirred a large pot of gravy at the stove while Aunt Pearl busied herself at the counter slicing Mom's special Christmas cake and arranging it onto a large platter. Aunt Pearl had stacked the platter with dozens of slices, enough for a small army. Enough to get them all stinking drunk too. Mom's Christmas cake oozed with booze.

Aunt Pearl knew that none of us would actually eat the cake.

Instead, we would divide and conquer, stashing our uneaten pieces in every nook and cranny of the dining room until we could retrieve and dispose of them later. It was kind of unfair to serve it to guests, but I'd leave that to Aunt Pearl. She had invited them after all.

Despite Mom's talents in the kitchen, her alcohol-laden Christmas cake was horrible. Mom didn't take criticism well, and we just didn't have the heart to tell her how bad it was. So year after year, we hid our intense dislike for the cake, and Mom made more and more of the stuff. She truly believed we couldn't get enough of it.

The West family Christmas cake recipe dated back to our British ancestors. It had been passed down for generations, along with the legend that the cake was the real reason no creatures were stirring the night before Christmas. Our ancient house had once harbored mice. That is, until Mom had rediscovered and resurrected the ancient family recipe about a decade ago. Suddenly, our mouse problem disappeared. Her cake had one redeeming factor: it was lethal to the poor little creatures.

It seemed wrong in so many ways to serve it to our unsuspecting guests.

This year was a little different. Mom hadn't made the cake ahead of time like she usually did. She had made it only this morning, too late to prevent our little mouse problem from returning. Our family mansion was old and drafty with plenty of ways for the critters to get inside and escape the cold weather.

I wrinkled my nose and padded by Mom and Aunt Pearl unnoticed. I had just opened the fridge to grab Dominic a Budweiser when I felt something brush against my shoulder. I saw a red flash from the corner of my eye and screamed.

"What the heck—" Aunt Pearl dropped her knife onto the counter and stumbled backward. "Geesh, Cen! You scared the living daylights out of me. What's the matter with you? You've never seen Santa before?"

"Uh...S-Santa?" I turned and stared at the tall but slightly underweight Santa-suited man standing in our kitchen. Was this the same

Santa from the snow globe sleigh? If so, he was just another one of Aunt Pearl's tricks. Somehow, she had managed to ruin all my childhood memories. Now, Santa was all creepy and stalker-like. Good thing we had no kids around because they would be traumatized forever.

My stare locked onto Santa's pale blue eyes and recognition set in. This was no apparition. It was Earl, Aunt Pearl's not-so-secret admirer. I hadn't recognized him in disguise at first, but that was understandable. He was a no-nonsense retired farmer that nobody ever expected to dress up as Santa Claus.

For some unfathomable reason, easy-going Earl liked ornery Aunt Pearl. His calm demeanor was the polar opposite of my cranky, conniving aunt. He seemed willing to go to great lengths to make her happy, which probably explained his Santa suit. That made me happy too. I liked Earl a lot, especially for the calming effect he had on Aunt Pearl.

Mom giggled. "You walked right past Earl, Cen. You're so lost in your own thoughts that you didn't see him."

Santa's eyes twinkled with amusement. "This suit is pretty flashy, Cen. Kind of hard to miss."

I was definitely preoccupied, wondering if Tyler was okay. "Uh, sorry, Earl. I wasn't expecting to see you." *Especially not in a baggy Santa Claus suit.* "Aunt Pearl said you weren't coming—"

"I said nothing of the sort," Aunt Pearl snapped. "Why don't you show Earl into the dining room?"

Once we were out of earshot Earl confided, "This whole Santa thing was Pearl's idea. To tell you the truth, I feel kind of silly in this getup. But if it keeps Pearl happy, it's worth it."

Amen to that.

Normally, I wouldn't have been surprised to see Earl. He lived nearby and had no place else to go on holidays. He had joined us for Thanksgiving dinner. But Aunt Pearl told us earlier that Earl had a new girlfriend and wasn't coming.

Another fib just for the fun of it. I never knew whether to believe Aunt Pearl or not.

"Let's go sit in the dining room." I beckoned for Earl to follow and grabbed a bottle of Witching Hour Red, a merlot vintage from our small onsite vineyard. As we entered the dining room no one mentioned Earl's Santa suit, making it all the more awkward. Obviously, they were at a loss for words.

Earl sat at the foot of the table. His seating choice was strategically beside Aunt Pearl's regular seat on his left. Her cane rested against the chair back despite her being in the kitchen. Her cane was really her wand, of course.

It was hard to know if Earl was truly ignorant or just wilfully blind to Aunt Pearl's witchy talents. Whatever the reason, he never questioned how she got around without her cane or noticed any of her frequent supernatural shenanigans. Love is blind, I guess.

My stomach growled despite the cake sighting. I placed the wine on the table and handed the Budweiser to Dominic. "I'm impressed that you came all the way from Vanuatu to surprise Merlinda."

"Yeah, well…" He twisted the cap off the beer bottle and downed a generous gulp. He slammed the bottle on the table and let out a sigh as he leaned back in his seat. He squeezed Merlinda's hand. "She's worth it."

I glanced outside and saw that the porch railing had disappeared under a pile of snow. Somehow, Dominic had made it through road closures and the blizzard of the century. And that was after leaving a tropical paradise just to surprise his girlfriend thousands of miles and half an ocean away for dinner. No man had ever done anything remotely close to that for me.

Not that I wanted Tyler to abandon stranded motorists, of course. As sheriff, he couldn't just up and leave simply because dinner beckoned. I kind of wished for it though. I also considered all the people out driving as inconsiderate. If they weren't out there getting stranded in the storm, then Tyler wouldn't be stuck rescuing them.

Maybe that was selfish, but was it so wrong to want my boyfriend by my side on Christmas Eve?

"You left the sun and sand for this weather? That must have been hard," Aunt Amber said.

"Not at all." Dominic wrapped his arm around Merlinda and squeezed her shoulder so hard that her chair tilted toward him on two legs. "Nothing could keep me away."

Merlinda steadied herself with a hand on the table. "Who's taking care of the dive shop? You left during the busy season."

"You have a dive shop?" Dominic didn't strike me as a sporty aquatic type. His muscle-bound body would sink like an anchor. Or maybe he would just use someone else as an anchor. His dive shop was probably a cover for drug smuggling or something equally nefarious and shady. There was something a little off about him, though I couldn't quite put my finger on it.

"Not my shop. I just work there." Dominic turned back to Merlinda. "Everything's cool, I got someone to take care of things while I'm gone. I missed you so much, babe. I just wanted to be with you for the holidays."

Dominic pried open Merlinda's palm and extracted the mistletoe. He placed it on the coffee table between their drinks. "You don't need lucky charms. I'm here to protect you, now and always."

Merlinda's expression darkened. She gulped her wine and deposited her wineglass on the table with so much force it spilled. Little red droplets stained the white tablecloth. "You were supposed to keep an eye on things. I thought we agreed—"

Dominic held a finger to his lips. "Shush, babe. We don't need to keep it a secret from them."

"Keep what a secret?" Mom emerged from the kitchen with a steaming dish of mashed potatoes. She placed the dish on the dining room table and wiped her hands on her apron.

"There are problems on Vanuatu. Merlinda has a price on her head," Dominic said.

Mom gasped. "Merlinda, you never told us you were in danger! Who on earth wants to hurt you?"

Merlinda shrugged. "Dominic is exaggerating. It's really not as bad as Dominic says."

Dominic shook his head. "No, you're not safe in Vanuatu. Not even here. That's why I came here to protect you."

"Protect Merlinda from what?" Mom asked. "Westwick Corners is the safest place around."

"Merlinda's enemies are hell-bent on getting to her. They want to harness her powers for John Frum and the cargo cult," Dominic said.

"Who's John Frum?" Aunt Amber asked.

Merlinda waved her hand in dismissal. "He's not a real person."

"Whatever the reason is, nobody's coming here anytime soon," Earl said. "We're smack dab in the middle of a blizzard for a while yet."

Merlinda glared at Earl. "You're not a weather expert."

Earl seemed completely oblivious to Merlinda's hatred of him. "Could've told you about this storm weeks ago. If you asked me I would have suggested you take an earlier flight. The Farmer's Almanac predicted lots of snow and a cold winter this year."

"Well, I didn't ask you, did I?" Merlinda rolled her eyes. "You actually believe in the Farmer's Almanac?"

Earl raised a brow. "Of course I believe in it. It's been right for the better part of the last fifty years, maybe longer."

"Earl's been farming for a long time," I said. Merlinda's rudeness was inexcusable, but I had to admit that I felt a small sense of satisfaction seeing a crack in Merlinda's perfect façade. Earl had just tried to be helpful, and she had practically bit his head off.

"Why are these people after you, dear?" Aunt Amber frowned. "Who is this John Frum guy? And what on earth is a cargo cult? Is it for people who love designer luggage? Or something to do with ocean travel?"

A faint smile crossed Merlinda's lips as she slowly shook her head. "I wish it was that simple."

Aunt Pearl stood just behind Merlinda, though I hadn't noticed her enter the dining room. She set the gravy boat carefully down on the table in front of Merlinda, like an offering to a goddess.

"Merlinda doesn't need your help, Dominic," Aunt Pearl snapped. "She's perfectly capable of taking care of herself."

"Now Pearl…" Earl's soothing voice had its effect, and everyone was silent for a moment.

Dominic sucked in his breath and frowned. "You didn't tell them anything, babe?"

"Tell us what?" Mom had missed part of the conversation while on another trip to the kitchen. This time she brought a basket of freshly baked buns. "I hope everybody's hungry. You can share your news over dinner."

"But Tyler isn't here yet." I glanced out the window, dismayed there was still no sign of his Jeep. Dominic's Escalade was already covered with a few inches of fresh snow, now a white lump in the unploughed driveway. "Can't we wait a few more minutes?"

"He's probably not coming, Cen." Aunt Pearl's eyes twinkled with mischief. "Ooh…I bet he got a better offer."

I opened my mouth to answer but stopped. Aunt Pearl liked to provoke me, but I wasn't taking the bait.

Mom shook her head. "I've held off as long as I could, dear. I guess Tyler's still stuck out there. I'll just warm up a plate for him when he gets here."

"Okay." I sighed, feeling sorry for myself. Just as well, I decided. With both Dominic and Merlinda here, things weren't even remotely like the special family Christmas Eve I had hoped for.

I glanced at the empty seat beside me and half-listened to the conversation. Mom and Aunt Pearl brought more steaming dishes out before taking their places at the table.

The table was crammed with bowls of vegetables, stuffing, cranberry sauce, and of course, the turkey. The two dozen or so dishes were more than enough to feed a coven of calorie-starved witches and then some.

But I had lost my appetite, worried that something had happened to Tyler. I called his cell phone but now he didn't answer.

Mom caught my eye and smiled in sympathy.

I smiled back, hoping my disappointment wasn't as obvious to everyone else. I dropped a warm bun onto my plate and passed the basket to Aunt Pearl. If I pretended to enjoy myself, then maybe I actually would.

I glanced around the table, noticing that Aunt Pearl in her green velvet pantsuit and Earl in his red velour Santa suit complemented each other in a weird sort of way. Aunt Pearl, with her gray hair and festive green velvet, resembled an anorexic elderly Mrs. Claus. Earl's red suit hung loosely on his large frame and gave him an aging hippie Santa look.

Aunt Amber spooned a generous helping of candied carrots onto her plate and passed the dish to Mom on her left. "I want the inside scoop on this cargo cult. Can anyone join?"

"There's no formal membership or anything. It's not that kind of cult," Merlinda said. "John Frum is mostly legend. Even if he was a real person, most of the stories about him are made-up. But on Vanuatu, people honestly believe that he has the power to bestow riches on true believers."

"Believers of what?" I half-listened as I watched the window for any sign of Tyler.

"It's mostly a myth that got kind of jumbled together over the years. Some real events got embellished because people wanted to believe they could bring it all back." Merlinda glanced at Dominic. "The U.S. Navy and other fleets stopped in Vanuatu during the Second World War. They had all sorts of gadgets the locals never even knew existed, like radios, watches, and other things. And amazing food and drink, like Spam and Coca-Cola."

"I wouldn't call Spam amazing," Earl turned to Merlinda on his right. "You gotta try some of my grain fed chicken..."

"You sold your farm, Earl. Remember?" Aunt Amber shifted her gaze to Dominic. "I guess they never had stuff like that in Vanuatu back then. It's harmless wishful thinking."

"Like Christmas and Santa Claus," Aunt Pearl added. "The story is part real and part pretend."

"Years ago you couldn't just order stuff online," Dominic said. "Especially not in Vanuatu. It's a remote group of islands in the middle of nowhere. Nothing but sand and palm trees."

Merlinda nodded. "The islanders thought that the strangers could magically conjure up all kinds of luxury goods and conveniences. Nobody on Vanuatu had ever seen those things before. That is, until the 1930's and 1940's when the US Navy used the islands as a World War II staging ground. When the servicemen left a few years later, people always expected that the American naval personnel would return."

"And bring back all the good stuff and good times," Dominic agreed. "Only they never did."

"Magic is what people call things they don't understand." I hoped the conversation was enough to distract from Aunt Pearl and whatever it was she had up her green velvet sleeve.

Merlinda nodded. "Vanuatu is hard to get to even today, and not many people visit. It's very expensive to ship stuff there. There are still plenty of things not available in Vanuatu that you can easily buy elsewhere. You can imagine how people's imaginations ran wild when strangers arrived with all kinds of modern conveniences they have never seen before. Cargo, in other words. The locals believed that all the goods were conjured up because they didn't know how else to explain it. That's why it's called a cargo cult."

"But weren't there other people on the ships besides John Frum? Why worship one man?" I asked.

Merlinda shrugged. "John Frum was just a composite of all the enlisted men that visited the islands in those days. When they all left after World War II ended, the locals channeled their energies into whatever they thought would bring the ships back. It was a collective wish that just grew bigger over the years."

"Bunch of crazies," Earl said. "Instead of wishful thinking, they could have grown their own food. Didn't they stop and think about it?"

"You can't grow Coca-Cola and Spam. What do you know anyway?" Merlinda scowled. "You've never been there. You've probably never even left Washington State."

Earl snorted. "Don't need to be a world traveler to know magical thinking when I see it."

Aunt Pearl frowned. "Now Earl...I think what Merlinda is trying to say is that she—"

"Merlinda! What's gotten into you?" Dominic shook his head. "Poor Earl was just asking a question."

"No, he's arguing with me like he always does." She turned to Earl. "Face it, Earl. Pearl doesn't like you and wants you to stop stalking her."

"I never said that, Merlinda." Aunt Pearl's face flushed crimson red, her skin contrasting against her green velvet pantsuit. The festive holiday mood from moments earlier evaporated.

Earl laughed. "You sure didn't, Pearl. I mean, you practically begged me to come for dinner."

That sounded far-fetched, but on the other hand, Aunt Pearl *had* invited other people, so Earl's claim held a grain of truth. She had never invited people to our house before. Yet here we were, with a bunch of unusual dinner guests on Christmas Eve. She was definitely up to something.

Mom changed the subject back to Vanuatu. "What does this cargo cult have to do with Merlinda?"

"Merlinda has special powers," Dominic said. "She makes things appear out of nowhere."

So Dominic knew Merlinda was a witch after all. Kind of obvious since she was a Pearl's Charm School student. He had probably figured out by now that we were witches too.

I glanced at Earl. If he knew anything about our witchy powers he never let on. But since he was constantly around Aunt Pearl, how could he not know?

"I don't know how Merlinda conjures up all that stuff, only that she does. It's pretty amazing. Oh, I almost forgot." Dominic reached into his pocket and handed her a small packet of dried herbs. "Your medicine."

"Thank goodness! I've been needing this." Merlinda opened the packet and sprinkled the entire contents onto her mashed potatoes. She mixed the green powder into the potatoes with a fork.

"Hey, what is that?" Earl pointed his fur-trimmed red velvet-clad arm at Merlinda's plate. His reach extended diagonally across the table and directly over Dominic's full plate. Earl squinted at Merlinda's potatoes. "Looks like marijuana."

Dominic swatted Earl's arm away. "Hey, get your arm out of my food." He leaned his shoulder in and blocked Earl's arm. "Have you ever seen weed, old man? It doesn't look anything like that."

Merlinda ignored them. She swallowed a spoonful of mashed potatoes and continued on with her story. "What I do isn't all that amazing, really. Pearl taught me that if you want something bad enough, you just focus the power of your mind on it, and your wishes will come true. That's basically all I do."

"Hear that, Cen?" Aunt Pearl pointed at me with her fork.

I scowled.

Aunt Pearl finally had the protégé she wanted. And probably a confidante too. Whether Merlinda's slight was intentional or not, I took it that way, a veiled reference to witchcraft and that I was a lousy witch simply because I didn't apply myself.

But that wasn't the reason at all. I've just always felt that my witchy talents gave me such an unfair advantage since most people couldn't cast spells. It felt like cheating somehow. At the same time, it seemed wrong to waste my natural talents. If I didn't have faith in myself, why would anyone else?

I could have used witchcraft to help Tyler finish his workday. That is, if I had learned the necessary spellcraft in the first place. Maybe it wasn't too late. I visualized Tyler on the highway, crouched against the wind as he grabbed the door handle of his Jeep. Then safely inside, turning the ignition…

"Cen?" Aunt Pearl's voice cut through my daydream.

"Huh?"

"Can you imagine the motivation you'd have if you lived in Vanu-atu?" Aunt Pearl said. "You'd have nothing to do all day but practice—"

I interrupted Aunt Pearl's attempt to change the subject. I worried that she'd expose us all as witches. "Vanuatu sounds like paradise."

"There are pros and cons. There's really not much to do there other than spin stories," Dominic said. "And drink and surf."

"And maybe practice a little witchcraft." Aunt Pearl batted her eyelashes in mock innocence.

Aunt Amber gasped, her fork poised in mid-air.

"Pearl!" Mom glared at her sister.

"I was just making small talk," Aunt Pearl said. "What's wrong with that?"

I noticed Aunt Pearl's long fake eyelashes for the very first time. She also wore green eyeshadow in the exact shade of her green velvet pantsuit. She never wore eye makeup, ever.

The only time she ever cared about her appearance was when she shape-shifted into Carolyn Conroe, her Marilyn Monroe alter ego. And that was always with the intent to trick people. Now that I thought of it, she hadn't shape-shifted in months. She seemed content, even happy, in her own skin.

It had to be the Earl effect. Aunt Pearl wouldn't have invited him and encouraged his attentions if she hadn't felt the same way he did. Maybe that was why Merlinda disliked him so much. Earl was Merlinda's competition for Aunt Pearl's affections. Kind of a weirdly unromantic love triangle.

Aunt Pearl suddenly dropped the mashed potatoes. But the dish didn't crash onto the table. Instead, it floated toward me and drifted just out of reach.

We had a standing agreement not to practice magic or talk about it in front of ordinary people. Yet Aunt Pearl had purposely flaunted it tonight, as if she dared us to say something.

Well, I wasn't going to give her the satisfaction of falling into her trap. Instead, I leaned forward and grabbed the dish. I pushed it down onto the table with a little more force than necessary. But dishes covered every inch of the table. Instead of landing on an empty spot, the dish hit the side of the gravy boat, tipping it over. Gravy spilled all over Mom's white linen tablecloth.

"Oh no! I'll grab a cloth." Aunt Amber bolted from her seat and headed into the kitchen. She returned minutes later and mopped up the mess. "Tell us more about this cargo cult."

"They really take the cargo cult seriously on Vanuatu," Dominic added. "There's a John Frum day every year. Locals dress like servicemen, complete with improvised U.S. Navy uniforms and fake weapons carved from wood. Most people just enjoy the celebration, but many others secretly believe that if they consistently perform the rituals, John Frum will return and bestow them with riches."

Merlinda waved her fork for emphasis. "People on Vanuatu still believe—or half-believe—in the supernatural. But the believers are in the minority now. That's a big problem for a few local leaders who claim to have a spiritual connection to John Frum. The myth is lucrative for them, so they scare people into following along. They keep their grip on power by making people believe that they have a special connection. They claim that when John Frum finally returns to Vanuatu, only the true believers will be rewarded."

"Like a religious messiah?" The dinner conversation was a lot more interesting than I had expected.

Dominic laughed. "It's hardly a religion. More like Santa Claus coming with presents for the kids than anything else, except John Frum day is on February 15th."

"Ooh, what fun! Valentine's Day and then John Frum day. Back to back holidays!" Aunt Amber downed her wine and placed her empty glass on the table.

Merlinda frowned but remained silent as she scooped mashed turnips onto her plate.

"What does all this have to do with you, Dominic?" I spooned out a generous helping of cranberry sauce onto my already-full plate.

"Nothing to do with me, but Merlinda is a real threat to them," Dominic said. "They know she's a witch. If she won't cooperate, they will disable her so she's not a threat to their lucrative existence."

So Dominic knew of Merlinda's supernatural abilities after all. Witches entrusted their secrets with only their closest friends and family, so their relationship must be serious.

"Cooperate how?" Mom asked.

Dominic sighed. "A couple of local leaders offered Merlinda a lot of money to conjure up some new trucks and computers."

"That's totally against WICCA rules." Unlike Aunt Pearl, Aunt

Amber did everything by the book—except when she had a little too much festive cheer. "I hope you didn't take them up on that offer."

"Of course not, Amber. I know the rules." Merlinda seemed insulted by Aunt Amber's insinuation.

Earl's face remained expressionless. If he was puzzled by the WICCA reference he didn't let on. He obviously had some inkling of our witchy ways but never asked questions. Maybe he didn't care. Or maybe he knew everything.

CHAPTER 6

"Tell us more about John Frum," Aunt Pearl said.

Merlinda nodded. "The myths are so old that I don't know much more than what I've already told you. The cult has been dying off in recent years."

"That's another reason they want Merlinda's help—to resurrect the myth with a new John Frum sighting," Dominic said. "Make everybody happy, and then politicians get re-elected. But we need to be the ones in charge. Merlinda keeps up the myth, and we can make some serious money too."

"What do you mean by 'we'?" I asked. "You're going to fake John Frum's return?" I liked Dominic even less now.

Dominic waved his hand in the air. "Nah. Just give the people what they want. Someone's going to do it anyway, so it might as well be us."

"But Merlinda's female," Aunt Amber protested. "She can't pass for a man."

"That's where I come in," Dominic said. "I'll wear a disguise and pass myself off as Frum. I'll distribute new trucks and TV's while Merlinda conjures them up behind the scenes. We'll sell them below market value and make a fortune."

"That way you get all the credit. Yet Merlinda does all the work," Aunt Amber said.

Merlinda shrugged. "I don't care about that, Amber. I'd just as soon not have to deal with all the attention."

"You would still profit from it, though. You just said that you wouldn't misuse your powers with the local leaders. I don't see how doing the same scheme with Dominic is any different." I abandoned all pretense of hiding our witchy secret. Everyone else was already giving it away, so it was impossible for me to do more harm.

"I'm not misusing anything," Merlinda said. "I'm just doing my own thing. There's nothing wrong with fulfilling people's wishes, is there? If Dominic wants to capitalize on it, I'm not going to stop him. I'm not doing that part, so I'm not breaking any WICCA rules. People can draw their own conclusions about John Frum."

"That's just a technicality." No one seemed to hear me.

"But if fulfilling wishes is the very thing that makes people come after you, then why keep doing it? Doesn't that just encourage them even more? No amount of money is worth fearing for your safety." Aunt Amber's innocent-sounding question was her way of getting to the details, to find an infraction, so she could shut the whole scheme down. Merlinda no longer seemed all that golden. Or maybe Dominic had her brainwashed.

"Gotta make a living somehow," Dominic said. "There aren't many jobs on Vanuatu. The dive shop barely breaks even. I could lose my job any day now."

There weren't a lot of jobs in Westwick Corners either. Yet we didn't go around conjuring up consumer goods. Even Aunt Pearl rarely worked the system to that extent.

"Aren't you just enriching yourselves at the expense of these poor people and their fantasies?" I asked. "They believe in something that's never going to happen."

"Not at all," Dominic said. "We're making their dreams a reality. We entertain them by giving them what they want. And if I pose as John Frum, it takes a lot of pressure off Merlinda."

"How selfless of you," Aunt Pearl snapped. She was jealous of Dominic. He had stolen the limelight, at least in her eyes.

"We give the local leaders what they want and everybody wins." He patted Merlinda's hand. "One of them is struggling to keep his grip on power. He doesn't want to be upstaged by a woman, either. I think we found the perfect solution."

And Pearl snorted. "Merlinda does all the work, and men take credit for it? You're just the latest one. I don't think so."

Dominic rolled his eyes. "John Frum has to be a man according to all the stories. Who cares about credit if we get rich? People can get new trucks, TV's, or whatever at a fraction of the price. Everybody's happy. People get a deal, Merlinda and I make a little money, and the local leaders take credit for John Frum's return. They can keep their grip on power."

Merlinda remained silent, content to let Dominic do all the talking.

"That's how it works, at least in theory. The leaders are dependent on Merlinda to stay in power. They need her to produce the luxury goods that keep everyone happy. But Merlinda isn't just a huge opportunity to them." Dominic took a deep breath. "She's also a threat. The leaders will lose their competitive edge if they lose control of Merlinda's talents to a rival. They can't assume Merlinda's continued loyalty. They plan to kidnap her to ensure an uninterrupted supply and a monopoly on the cargo cult."

"The leaders can't force Merlinda to work against her will. Don't they have labor laws on Vanuatu?" Aunt Amber turned to Merlinda. "You can't go back there, dear. You have to stay here for your own safety."

Merlinda nodded but didn't say anything.

For such a powerful witch, Merlinda was sure acting helpless. She seemed content to let Dominic make money off her and for the local leaders to use her magic. Even Aunt Pearl wanted to keep Merlinda at Pearl's Charm School forever. Yet Merlinda had the power to stop it—if she really wanted to.

"Merlinda really is in a lot of trouble," Dominic said. "The rivalry between the leaders is so great that one of them might even kill Merlinda just to prevent the other from harnessing her powers. That's where I come in. I keep Merlinda safe and them happy at the same time."

"It sounds so dangerous." Mom gasped and her hand flew to her chest. "Why do you two have to go back there at all? You can both get jobs somewhere else."

Aunt Pearl scratched her chin. "You can stand up to those bullies. Beat them at their own game."

I shot a warning glance at Aunt Pearl. She was a little too ready to stir up trouble.

Aunt Amber sighed. "At least you're safe here. I see why you want to go back though. Home is home, and your friends and family are all there. Speaking of family, does anyone else in your family have these special talents?"

Merlinda shrugged. "I'm an only child, the only one in my family with the powers. My mother had them, but she's gone now."

"Can't the police protect you from these men?" I asked.

"I wish." Merlinda shook her head slowly. "One of the leaders is the chief of police. The other is the mayor, so that doesn't help me any. Both are perpetuating the John Frum legend. If I don't help them, they risk me exposing their trickery. I can prove the cult is a sham."

Mom sighed. "You poor thing. Isn't there someone else in Vanuatu that can help you?"

"Not really," Merlinda said. "The chief of police just happens to be my father."

CHAPTER 7

e were still discussing Merlinda's cargo cult dilemma when the doorbell rang.

My heart skipped a beat. Tyler was finally here!

I raced to the front door and threw it open. Relief flooded over me as I stared into Tyler's warm brown eyes. His damp ski jacket was unzipped, revealing his sheriff's uniform underneath. His khaki pants were soaked to the knees from the snow, and he looked exhausted.

And drop dead sexy, even soaking wet.

As I pulled him close and kissed him, his five-o'clock shadow tickled my chin. "I was so worried about you. I tried calling and… thank goodness you made it."

He grinned. "Sorry, my phone died. I thought I'd never get here. I've been looking forward to dinner all day. Is Pearl behaving so far?"

I nodded. "She's preoccupied. Merlinda missed her flight today, and we also have an unexpected guest." I filled him in as I took his coat and hung it on the coatrack. With all the distractions and the festive season, I hoped Aunt Pearl wouldn't taunt Tyler like she usually did.

Tyler tilted his head toward the door. "That explains the Escalade. Anyone I know?"

I shook my head. "Merlinda's boyfriend, Dominic, drove all the way from Shady Creek after flying in from Vanuatu for an unannounced visit. Aunt Pearl had invited him as a surprise for Merlinda, except she didn't tell us, either. But the weird thing is that Merlinda wasn't supposed to be here. Her flight was canceled at the last minute because of the storm."

"Vanuatu's in the South Pacific, right?"

I nodded. "Dominic is um…a regular guy." Tyler knew we were witches. He had to know that Merlinda was one too since she attended Pearl's Charm School. Like most locals, Tyler hadn't interacted much with Merlinda because she kept to herself and rarely went into town.

Tyler chuckled. "Pearl really invited him? Since when does Pearl throw a party?"

"Since now." I squeezed his arm and pulled him toward me for another kiss. "You'll have to see it to believe it. Oh, and Earl's here."

Tyler grinned. "Oh good. Another normal guy so I'm not outnumbered."

I jumped as a woman's voice warbled behind me. "Woo-hoo! This hottie just made my night a whole lot better." She let out a low whistle.

I had completely forgotten about ghostly Grandma Vi. It always disturbed me that she liked Tyler almost as much as I did.

Tyler felt me flinch. "Why are you so jumpy?"

I pulled back from Tyler's embrace and shrugged. He couldn't see or hear Grandma Vi, and explaining my ghostly grandma only invited more questions than answers. He knew we were witches but had no idea that our family matriarch lingered on as a ghost long after her passing. I hated keeping secrets from him. On the other hand, her silly crush and constant presence whenever he was around was a little disturbing to say the least.

"I was so worried about you out in the snowstorm," I said. "And then Dominic arrived. To be honest, Merlinda's boyfriend scares me. I guess I'm a little on edge."

Grandma floated a few feet above us. "Tyler can protect us from that gangster. I still can't believe you let that ruffian in here."

"I had no choice—" I stopped mid-sentence.

"Huh?" Tyler frowned.

"Aunt Pearl is up to something," I said. "She didn't invite Dominic out of the goodness of her heart. She's planning something. What exactly, I don't know."

I just hoped things didn't spiral out of control.

Tyler chuckled. "I can't wait to see what Pearl has in store. It could take the heat off me for a change."

Aunt Pearl despised Tyler. She had stepped up her pyromania since he became sheriff. Her attempts to drive him out of town never worked. He always held her to account for her shenanigans with hefty fines, and occasionally, public shaming. No one else kept her in check the way he did, and she resented his power over her.

"You are the heat, sonny." Grandma floated behind Tyler. She leered at his backside with approval. "If I was a little younger, I'd go for you myself."

"Stop it!" I glared at Grandma Vi and made a zipping motion across my lips.

"Stop what? I'm not doing anything." Tyler's brows furrowed together. "Why are you acting so weird?"

"Sorry. It's just been a long day." Even with Tyler finally here, my hoped-for perfect Christmas Eve wasn't going to happen. While I was relieved and happy at Tyler's safe arrival, I didn't want our time together to be full of distractions, entertaining guests, or anything else.

Grandma Vi puckered her lips and blew me a kiss, mocking me in a way that only ghosts can.

I ignored her, distracted by the howling wind that sprayed snow across the threshold. I had been so thrilled to see Tyler that I had forgotten to shut the door. I slammed it shut. "Forget about Aunt Pearl. I'm just glad you finally made it."

He wrapped his arms around my waist and pulled me into a long, slow kiss. "I've been looking forward to this all day."

"Bravo." Grandma Vi hovered a few feet away from us and clapped.

At least Tyler's arrival had pulled Grandma Vi out of her depression. She always got a little melancholy around Christmastime. The holidays reminded her of days gone by, and that we were no longer flush with cash.

Operating the inn wasn't necessarily a bad thing. The bed and breakfast kept us all busy and out of trouble for the most part. We met new people and kept the town's economy going. The income allowed us a comfortable existence without having to commute to jobs in bigger communities as many of our neighbors did. It was really the best of both worlds.

But ghosts don't need money and Grandma Vi just wanted her house back. Now, the one week we were closed for the season had been invaded by strangers too. Dominic wasn't even a paying guest.

For tonight at least, I shared Grandma Vi's feelings. It was Christmas Eve, after all. At least Tyler's presence was one small consolation for her. She adored Tyler, even though he didn't know she existed.

Grandma Vi's face brightened as if she had read my mind. In fact, she had. Mind reading was one of her supernatural talents.

Her smile was contagious. Before I could stop myself, I was smiling too.

"What's so funny?" Tyler followed my gaze. "Too much holiday cheer already?"

Grandma Vi wiggled her finger. "Ooh! Somebody's got a secret. Does Ruby know how hot and heavy you two are? Maybe he'll pop the question tonight."

Of course Mom knew. Grandma just wanted to provoke a reaction from me. I held up my arm, palm outwards, traffic cop style. "Just stop it."

"Stop what?" Tyler scanned the hallway, frowning when he didn't see anyone. "Is this more of your weird family stuff?"

"Um, yeah…something like that. Why don't you head into the dining room? We just sat down to eat. I'll be there in a sec."

"Oh. Okay." Disappointment flashed across his face.

Great. Now Tyler thought I was annoyed with him. I waited until he was out of earshot. "Cut it out, Grandma."

Grandma Vi clasped her hands together. "Such a nice young man, and you're so grumpy. Don't let him get away, Cen. You would make such a sweet couple!"

"We already are a couple. And you're nuts." I turned away from Grandma Vi and headed to the dining room.

She trailed after me, her ghostly aura a mix of angry orange and reds. "You're calling me crazy? My granddaughter, my own flesh and blood, hurling insults when all I want to do is make friends—"

"You're overreacting, Grandma. You know I didn't mean it like that." I stopped in the living room, determined to end our spat before we reached everyone in the dining room. "Let's go eat."

"I'm a ghost, Cen. You know I can't eat. Stop taunting me!" She rubbed her stomach with a transparent hand.

"Sorry, Grandma. I just meant that I'll miss you if you don't join us at the table."

We both jumped as a gust of wind blew the front door open. The door thudded against the wall before half closing again.

I ran to the door, certain I had closed it.

A woman's voice froze me in my tracks. It wasn't the wind after all.

CHAPTER 8

"Wait!" A bleach-blonde in a black leather jacket waved to me as she walked briskly across the driveway. Her sequined miniskirt ended just a few inches below her jacket hem, exposing chubby legs. Her only weather-appropriate attire was her snow boots. Judging by her awkward gait, they were too big and borrowed. An oversized red leather purse was slung over her shoulder. She carried a pair of red patent pumps in one hand and a bottle of wine in the other.

"Can I help you?" I stepped onto the porch and closed the front door behind me. I stood there shoeless, my arms crossed against the biting wind and frigid temperature.

"You better believe you can help me. You must be Cen." She paused at the bottom of the steps and let out an enormous sigh. She just stood there, as if she expected me to descend the stairs to meet her.

I didn't. "That's me. Do I know you?"

She climbed the stairs without answering. She shoved a bottle into my arms. "Here, take this."

I took the bottle as she passed me, spraying snow all over my stocking feet. I recognized the label. It was a cheap white wine popular at gas stations and 24-hour convenience stores, probably a last-minute purchase though it wasn't even chilled.

I had never seen her before, and Westwick Corners was so small that I knew everyone in town. I even knew most of the locals' out-of-town guests too. Most of those guests hadn't even made it into town because of the snowstorm. Yet here she was, acting like she owned the place.

I followed behind her as she waited expectantly at the front door.

Bleach-blondie reached the front door and stomped the snow off her boots. She waited impatiently for me to open the door. "You gonna let me in? I gotta get inside and warmed up."

"Oh my!" Grandma Vi hovered beside me. "I don't like the looks of this tart."

I glared at Grandma Vi before turning to the woman. "Thanks. The wine looks lovely. Are you a friend of—?"

She held out her hand. "I'm Gail. Didn't Brayden tell you I was coming?"

"Wait—what?" I shook her hand and turned. A man hurried across the driveway. My heart sank as I recognized Brayden, my ex-fiancé. Surely, he knew that his standing invitation to the West family Christmas Eve dinner had ended with our broken engagement earlier this year. Brayden was self-centered, but even he wasn't that dense.

Or maybe he did know and decided to show up anyway. With a date, no less. Knowing him, he probably wanted to make me jealous. Or, at the very least, show off a date since I would be with Tyler.

Brayden waved and quickened his pace. "Hey, Cen. I see you've already met my girlfriend, Gail." He emphasized the last three words for effect.

"I uh…wasn't expecting you. What are you doing here?" As Westwick Corners' mayor, Brayden was also Tyler's boss. I doubted that his visit was anything work-related. Gail's wine bottle confirmed that. My Christmas Eve worsened by the minute.

"Pearl didn't tell you? She invited me—I mean us." He clamped a hand on Gail's shoulder. "Let's get inside. It's freezing cold out here."

Grandma Vi perked up as Gail and Brayden walked past her into the hallway. She started singing a Shania Twain song. "It's gonna be a party, uh-huh…"

"Grandma, stop that!" My whisper was just loud enough to stop Brayden in his tracks. He turned around.

"Still talking to yourself, I see." Brayden tossed their coats onto the hallway staircase banister. He turned and smirked before following Gail into the dining room.

I shut the door and leaned against it. Aunt Pearl was definitely up to something. I was beyond furious at her for inviting all these people. She had suddenly morphed from anti-social to party planner, inviting people I did not want to spend even a minute with. Maybe that was the party theme, given the arrival of my ex-fiancé and his strange new girlfriend.

"It's not all about you, Cen." Grandma Vi intruded into my thoughts. "Lighten up."

Maybe our strange roster of guests was Aunt Pearl's attempt at comedy. Witch games were a family tradition on Christmas Eve. We cast mischievous spells and tried to out-witch each other with supernatural high jinks. But we never involved ordinary people. I worried that Aunt Pearl was about to take things a little too far.

I headed into the dining room and placed Gail's gas station wine on the table. My dream Christmas was shaping up to be a bit of a nightmare, and it would only get worse.

And there was absolutely nothing I could do about it.

Even if the last person I wanted to spend Christmas Eve with was the man I had left at the altar. Even if he had the nerve to bring his new girlfriend. Even if my romantic dream Christmas was ruined.

And even though I knew Aunt Pearl had something up her sleeve, I was powerless to stop it.

CHAPTER 9

The conversation around the dinner table was awkward and stilted with our strange assortment of guests. Aunt Pearl had insisted Gail and Brayden sit opposite Tyler and me, so we had to stare across the table at one another all night long. Her seating arrangement was no doubt designed to stir up trouble between my current and former beaus.

Aunt Amber sat on Tyler's left and Aunt Pearl flanked my right in kind of an aunt sandwich.

Merlinda sat on Brayden's left. Dominic sat beside Merlinda with Santa-clad Earl on his other side at the foot of the table. Mom was at the head of the table nearest to the kitchen door.

Gail's smile from moments earlier had been replaced by a frown. She was fixated on Merlinda and not in a good way. At first, she stole sideways glances, but now it was a full-on glare. No wonder, since Brayden was staring unabashedly at Merlinda.

While I couldn't blame Gail for being jealous, her reaction seemed a bit obsessive. Her eyes flashed with hatred as she watched Merlinda's every move. Trouble was brewing. In fact, it was almost at the boiling point.

Brayden's enjoyment at being wedged between the two women was obvious. Even so, he remained completely oblivious to Gail's worsening mood as he helped himself to a freshly baked bun.

"Red or white?" Earl opened the red wine and poured glasses of merlot, followed by the white wine, a Sauvignon Blanc. I opted for the red as did everyone else except Gail, Brayden, and Merlinda, who chose the white.

Dominic shook his head and tapped his bottle. "I'll stick with beer."

Earl finished pouring the wine before helping himself to the eggnog. "I'm going to try some of Amber's concoction. From what I can see, it's got a bit of punch to it."

Aunt Amber giggled and raised her glass in a mock toast. "It's got a kick, all right."

Aunt Pearl was unusually chatty, boasting about Merlinda's academic achievements, though in nonspecific terms. She was no doubt trying to guilt me into returning to Pearl's Charm School. Well, I wasn't taking the bait.

As Aunt Pearl droned on and on about Merlinda, my thoughts drifted.

Gail lifted her wineglass to her lips and just as quickly slammed it down on the table, spilling wine everywhere.

I was jolted back to reality as I watched an enraged Gail from across the table. Someone, or something, had upset her, though I had been too distracted to notice. Whatever it was had triggered Gail's anger. She was a lit fuse ready to explode at any moment. I wanted to say something, but no one else seemed to notice her but me.

Aunt Pearl patted my hand, seemingly oblivious to Gail's anger. "All you have to do is apply yourself, Cen. No need to be a dropout. School's not that hard."

Gail interrupted before I got a chance to answer. She leaned forward and stared sideways at Merlinda. "What exactly are *you* studying here in Westwick Corners, Merlinda?"

"Um...philosophy and mysticism," Merlinda said.

Brayden shifted uncomfortably in his seat.

I doubted his discomfort stemmed from either Gail's bad vibes or the mystical references. He was generally oblivious to other people's feelings. More than likely, it was because no one had passed him the turkey platter yet.

"There's no university here in Westwick Corners," Gail pointed out. "Where are you going to school?"

Despite my feelings about Merlinda, I felt a need to butt in. "Merlinda's researching her thesis. What are you doing here, Gail?"

Mom's mouth dropped open. "What Cen means is—"

"I've never seen you in town before, Gail," I went on. "Did you just move here?" It was possible that I hadn't noticed her in Westwick Corners because Brayden was purposely avoiding me. On the other hand, Brayden had brought Gail to our family Christmas Eve celebration. Hardly avoidance. No, he was too self-centered to even register my feelings as a social faux pas. He did notice one person, though.

Merlinda. Brayden just couldn't take his eyes off her. If she wasn't such a recluse, he likely would have met her around town earlier. And maybe things would have been a lot less awkward.

Gail shook her head. "Uh, no. I live in Shady Creek. Brayden and I usually hang out there. We couldn't make it back to Shady Creek with the highway closed, so Pearl insisted we come here for dinner…"

"Glad we did." Brayden's voice trailed off as he gazed trancelike at Merlinda.

I turned to Tyler. He seemed oblivious to Merlinda's charms.

"Brayden said the roads were too dangerous. Right, Bray?" Gail craned her neck to get Brayden's attention, but it was no use.

By now Brayden was openly gawking at Merlinda. He was completely turned around in his chair, and his backside faced Gail.

For a moment, I thought Brayden's over the top obsession was some of Aunt Pearl's witchery, but even she shook her head in disgust.

Dominic noticed Brayden's fixation too. Dominic's face flushed with anger, though he tried hard to contain himself. He guzzled what remained of his beer and slammed the bottle down on the table.

"Bray? I asked you a question." Gail laser-focused on Brayden first, then Dominic. "What's wrong with you guys?"

Things were quickly deteriorating. Gail was a powder keg, ready to explode. I had to somehow diffuse the situation, but how?

"Brayden's got other things on his mind besides you, Gail," Aunt Pearl said. "He didn't hear a word you said."

"Aunt Pearl!" I glared at her, furious at her attempt to stir up trouble.

She smiled sweetly at me and patted her lips with a napkin.

"Brayden!" Gail yanked on Brayden's shoulder. "Look at me!"

As Brayden turned away from Merlinda, his elbow hit his wineglass, spilling white wine all over the tablecloth.

"Now look what you've done," Gail exclaimed. "A full glass of wine, wasted!"

Brayden shook his head. "If you hadn't grabbed my shoulder…"

Nobody dared mention that Gail had spilled her own wine just moments earlier. You could literally cut the tension in the room with a knife. Even Grandma Vi picked up on the vibe. She hovered above Gail's head, butter knife in hand.

"What the heck—?" Gail's hand flew to her hair. "Something just landed on my head." She brushed a glob of butter from her hair as she stared up at the ceiling.

Grandma Vi, invisible as always, giggled. Then Aunt Pearl laughed, followed by Aunt Amber. Everyone erupted into peals of laughter.

Except me.

And Gail.

She frowned as she studied the blob in the palm of her hand. "How the hell did this get in my hair? It looks like melted butter."

Aunt Pearl snorted. "I can't believe it's not butter."

"I know whose buns I'd like to butter." Grandma Vi's inappropriate comment at least brought Aunt Amber to her senses.

Aunt Amber gasped. "Sorry, dear. I accidentally flicked it off my knife when I buttered my bun. Fun fact: I think it's good for your skin."

"My skin doesn't need anything extra. Somebody pass me the buns." Gail's frown deepened. She scanned up and down the table looking for the dinner rolls. Her eyes stopped on Brayden, who had just picked up the breadbasket.

Brayden's eyes were locked on Merlinda as he held out the breadbasket with two hands like a love-struck butler. He sucked in his breath as she extended a tawny manicured hand and delicately selected a bun.

Conversation around the table stopped as the silent drama unfolded.

I half-expected Brayden to bow or kiss Merlinda's hand, except he was seated and already had his hands full with the breadbasket.

Gail cleared her throat and glared at Brayden's back. Her face flushed as she waited for Brayden to turn back around and pass her the dinner rolls.

Instead, Brayden nodded sweetly at Merlinda and set the breadbasket down on the table.

Gail cleared her throat. "You didn't hear a word I said. Did you, Brayden?"

"Huh?" Brayden's expression was kind of a scared deer-in-the-headlights look.

My normally confident ex-boyfriend was afraid of Gail. I had never seen him that way before, and it worried me.

"Never mind. I'll do it myself." Gail reached in front of Brayden and grabbed the bun basket. "You're making a fool of yourself."

I kind of knew where Gail was coming from. It wasn't witchcraft or even feminine wiles. But whatever it was, men simply melted in Merlinda's presence. Even more maddening than them falling under her spell was that she seemed completely oblivious to their weird behavior. That's how life was for beautiful people. They were so used to dealing with legions of admirers that they remained unaware of their special treatment.

I wouldn't know. Though I managed to turn a few heads when I wore makeup and a curvy dress, it paled in comparison to the reaction Merlinda got. I sensed that most men would do just about anything to get her attention. And I mean anything—short of a felony. She was simply that drop-dead gorgeous.

I refocused on Gail, who, by now, looked ready to punch someone. Instead, she poured herself some merlot. She downed the glass within minutes. Then she leaned back in her chair and sighed. She was beaten, and she knew it.

Brayden stared at Merlinda, his empty fork midway between plate and mouth.

"Some wine?" Hoping to lighten the mood, Aunt Amber had left the table and returned with a fresh bottle of merlot. She filled Gail's empty wineglass first, and then continued around the table.

Aunt Amber's strategy was brilliant: eliminate the friction by getting Gail so drunk that she didn't care anymore.

Grandma Vi, hovered behind me, still fixated on Gail. "This woman is all wrong for Brayden."

"Since when do you care?" The words came out before I could stop them. Grandma Vi had never liked Brayden much in the first place, so her disapproval of Gail as a suitable partner for Brayden surprised me.

"What?" Tyler paused, his glass halfway to his mouth. "Who are you talking to?"

Brayden rolled his eyes. "You haven't noticed? She does that all the time."

Gail's face turned crimson as she glared at me. "Why are you staring at me like that?"

I avoided her gaze. "Sorry. I was just thinking out loud." I couldn't talk to Grandma Vi in front of the guests. I was dying to ask what she meant about Gail, but that would have to wait for later.

Grandma Vi hummed "Whose Bed Have Your Boots Been Under" as she danced back and forth above the carrots and mashed potatoes. She really was obsessed with Shania Twain.

Aunt Amber, Aunt Pearl, and Mom burst into peals of laughter.

Grandma Vi's Shania renditions amused me too, but I was determined not to show it.

"What's so funny?" Gail looked around her. "Why are you all staring at me?"

"We're not looking at you, dear," Mom said. "At least, not intentionally. It's just an old West family joke."

"Well, it's not funny," Gail snapped.

We all sat in awkward silence.

"Oh, my goodness," Mom exclaimed. "With all the guests, I really should have put out more turkey. There's more in the kitchen. I just need to carve it."

"I'll do it." Brayden jumped up from his chair, eager to escape Gail's wrath. He followed Mom into the kitchen.

Gail scanned our faces. She stood and dropped her napkin on her empty plate. She trailed behind them. "I'll help."

"Wait for me!" Grandma Vi spun around and floated behind them belting out another Shania Twain tune. "Ooh, there's gonna be a party!"

I rose from my chair and headed to the kitchen. Trouble was brewing with Grandma Vi's pranks, Gail's obsessive jealousy, and Brayden's hands on a carving knife.

Gail paused in the doorway. She turned and glared at me. "I don't know what you're up to, but you better stop right now."

I was speechless.

That was a good thing in this case, because I already had the sinking feeling that I was about to do something I would regret later. One way or another, we were headed for trouble, and I wasn't sure I could stop it.

CHAPTER 10

*B*rayden set to work carving the turkey under Gail's watchful gaze. Aunt Pearl and I observed from across the large kitchen island, careful to keep a safe distance from our psycho guest in case she went off the rails.

Gail stared daggers at me. I smiled politely in return, relieved she wasn't the one with a knife in her hand. I hadn't done anything to deserve her anger, but as Brayden's ex-girlfriend, maybe it was the mere fact that I existed in the first place. With Merlinda still in the dining room, I was now Gail's closest target. I knew better than to mess with a half-drunk, insanely jealous girlfriend.

Mom smiled at Gail. "Too bad you're missing your family back in Shady Creek. I know it's not quite the Christmas Eve you and Brayden expected."

"No big deal." Gail didn't elaborate further. She walked toward us and looked back and forth between Aunt Pearl and the Christmas cake. "Mmm…that cake looks good. Can I try some?"

"Of course." Aunt Pearl grinned and turned the platter around so that the largest piece of cake faced Gail. "Help yourself."

It worked. Gail took the bait.

That was mean of Aunt Pearl because nobody could stomach that cake. Nobody deserved it either. I opened my mouth to protest, but something stopped me. One bite of Mom's vile-tasting cake would stop Gail in her tracks without a word from me.

It didn't though. She ate the whole slice, and even helped herself to a second piece of the alcohol-laden cake.

"Don't eat too much, or you'll ruin your appetite." Mom was practically giddy over Gail's cake infatuation.

"It'll ruin a lot more than her appetite," Grandma Vi floated just behind Mom's shoulder, a transparent finger to her mouth in a mock gag gesture.

Aunt Pearl made a cutting motion across her neck.

Grandma Vi pouted. "Don't disrespect me, Pearl."

Luckily Mom was so focused on Gail that she missed Grandma Vi's cake insult.

I glared at Grandma Vi.

Gail scowled, assuming my hostile expression was directed at her.

Mom pointed to Gail's hand. "That cake always disappears faster than I can make it. I should have made more!"

Aunt Pearl snorted. "Too bad Christmas comes just once a year."

Mom smiled. "I can make the cake anytime you like, Pearl. All you have to do is ask. We don't have to wait for Christmas."

"No!" I said a little too forcefully. "Once a year keeps it special. We don't want to spoil the West family Christmas tradition."

I watched Gail polish off her second piece of cake, thinking how odd it was that she and Brayden were even here in the first place. Brayden's family lived out of state, and he always visited them for the holidays. Maybe they had planned to visit Gail's family in Shady Creek instead. But if that was the case, why hadn't they left for Shady Creek this morning before the highway closed?

The bigger question was why Gail had ever considered a Christmas Eve celebration with me, Brayden's ex-fiancée. Unless Brayden had neglected to tell her about me in the first place. That made sense, given how self-centered he could be.

I guessed that for whatever reason, Brayden hadn't wanted to spend the holiday with Gail's family. He could have purposely delayed their departure. And since Gail was insanely jealous, she was probably afraid to leave him on his own for Christmas. Maybe her sole reason to stay in town was just to keep an eye on Brayden.

By now I was certain Aunt Pearl was up to no good. If she had invited Brayden to join us only hours ago at the very last minute, then she knew Gail was part of the deal.

Mom turned from the sink and beamed at Gail. "I'm so glad you love the cake! I would love to give you the recipe, but I can't. It's a family secret. You'll never find another cake like it."

"That's for sure," Aunt Pearl said.

We all pretended to like Mom's cake so much that we had convinced her not to share the family recipe with outsiders. It was for general public safety reasons more than anything else. The downside was that Mom baked even more of her secret recipe each year, mistakenly believing that we all loved it.

The strangest thing was that Mom was an accomplished gourmet cook and a master baker. Everything else she made was mouth-watering delicious. Yet she was taste-blind when it came to her horrible Christmas cake. No one had the heart to tell her the truth. It was all we could do to prevent her from serving it to our bed and breakfast guests. Yet against all odds, Gail seemed to like it.

"Turkey's carved." Brayden held up the platter for all to see, proud of himself.

Mom beamed. "Looks wonderful, Brayden. Now, let's go eat. Cen, grab some more wine."

I grabbed another bottle of merlot and a bottle of white, a nice sauvignon blanc from a nearby estate winery.

Gail followed suit and grabbed two more bottles of white from our wine rack. Apparently, she was committed to getting drunk. I couldn't really blame her with Brayden's wandering eye. Spending Christmas Eve with his ex-girlfriend was bad enough. I just hoped that Gail wasn't a mean drunk.

Brayden held the door open for Mom and ushered her through to the dining room. Gail trailed behind, followed by Brayden with the turkey platter.

I waited until the door closed and turned to Aunt Pearl. "It was supposed to be a family dinner."

Aunt Pearl snorted. "Oh, just relax, Cen. Brayden is practically family."

"No, he isn't," I hissed. "He's been ex-family ever since we broke up. Why did you invite him in the first place? You don't even like him." Her plans to drive a wedge between Tyler and me were glaringly obvious.

Aunt Pearl rolled her eyes. "If it wasn't for that dead body at your wedding rehearsal, Brayden would be your husband right now. You know, technically you're both still single. It's not too late to turn things around."

"That's not going to happen." My almost-wedding to Brayden had been halted for good reason, and it wasn't because of a pre-marital murder. We simply weren't right for each other. My last-minute wedding jitters had stopped me from marrying the wrong man.

"Brayden's got a lot more going for him than what's-his-name," Aunt Pearl pointed out.

"You know Tyler's name. Even if you don't like him, you could at least be polite."

Aunt Pearl's face suddenly brightened. She grabbed the cake platter. "Why don't I offer Tyler some Christmas cake? You know, like a peace-offering."

"Don't you dare, Aunt Pearl. Poor Tyler is exhausted from work, and that cake has so much booze in it that he's liable to pass out." I knew better than to argue because she somehow sucked me in every time.

Grandma Vi snorted. "Did you see Gail? She already ate two pieces! That girl's got to have a strong constitution because she's still standing. Somebody better have a heart-to-heart with Ruby about her damn cake, though. She's liable to kill somebody."

"You could have told her years ago," I whispered. Grandma Vi wanted one of us to take the fall, as usual. The Christmas cake had been a tradition for years, so confronting Mom after all this time was too little, too late. Our big family conspiracy had backfired in our faces.

Grandma Vi shrugged. "Too late now. I'm a ghost. I can't eat anymore, so it's not my problem."

"It's all of our problem, Grandma. No wonder it's a secret recipe. It should stay that way." The family recipe had probably been passed down to Mom from Grandma Vi in the first place.

Grandma Vi shook her head. "It certainly didn't come from me, and there's nothing I can do about it. I do have a problem with all these guests, though. I could do something about that."

"No," I said. "They'll be gone in a few hours. Or at least by tomorrow morning when the storm lets up."

"That's far too long. How can I possibly relax with all these people here?" Grandma Vi hovered by the dining room door.

Aunt Pearl scowled. "Is it a crime to get into the holiday spirit?"

"No, but you're definitely up to something, Pearl," Grandma Vi said. "You hate people, and you hate socializing. You invited all these interlopers for a reason. I just wish I knew what it was."

I felt a presence behind me and turned to see Gail. I had no idea how long she had stood in the doorway.

Gail frowned as she eyed Aunt Pearl and me. "Who are you two talking to?"

"No one in particular." Aunt Pearl fake-smiled.

I waved a hand in dismissal. "Aunt Pearl was talking, not me. She talks to herself a lot. Senility and old age, I guess."

"Watch your mouth, missy. I'm sharper than everyone here." Aunt Pearl said.

Brayden came up behind Gail to see what all the fuss was about. He shook his head in disappointment at Aunt Pearl and me. "Can't you two just get along for once?"

My business hadn't been his business ever since we broke up. I opened my mouth to give him a piece of my mind but stopped short as Aunt Pearl's plans became clear. She was purposely provoking me into a fight by inviting Brayden and Gail in the first place. All because she resented me dating Tyler. Only her plan wasn't working, and she was frustrated.

Tyler was the first sheriff to stand up to Aunt Pearl and her arsonist antics. As my boyfriend, he was around way more often than she wanted. No wonder she'd rather see me with Brayden than Tyler, who she considered her archenemy.

I was a pawn in Aunt Pearl's chess game, and so was Tyler. Brayden, as my ex-fiancée and Tyler's boss as mayor, was Aunt Pearl's checkmate. Brayden's jealous girlfriend was a last-minute bonus, all designed to stir up trouble.

Add in the gorgeous Merlinda and it was clear that Aunt Pearl wanted all of us to be throwing pitchforks at each other. Well, I wasn't falling for it. This was just her latest attempt to make Tyler quit his sheriff post and leave town for good. Not if I could help it.

Brayden steered Gail back into the dining room and motioned for us to follow. "C'mon. Time to eat."

"Good idea." I smiled and shooed Aunt Pearl through the dining room doorway. "Let's go enjoy dinner."

Breaking bread together on a holiday could mend both old wounds and new. Brayden and I could be civil with one another, for starters. And while I didn't exactly expect Aunt Pearl and Tyler to become fast friends anytime soon, maybe we could plant the seed. It was worth a shot.

Aunt Pearl eyed me suspiciously, but she complied.

"Let them eat cake!" Grandma Vi squealed in delight as she clapped her hands together. "This is going to be good."

I opened my mouth to reply but caught myself just in time.

Tonight wasn't exactly the Christmas Eve I had planned, but it *was* getting interesting. I might as well sit back and enjoy the entertainment.

CHAPTER 11

The storm battled on but indoors all was calm after a delicious turkey dinner. Whatever jealousies simmered had been softened with copious amounts of alcohol.

We were all a little tipsy from too much good cheer. We had polished off a half-dozen bottles of wine between us, and Dominic had downed at least a half-dozen beers. Aunt Amber and Earl had enjoyed several generous glasses of spiked eggnog, and everyone was happy, or at least civil, to one another.

The alcohol had taken the edge off our personality conflicts and romantic rivalries for the moment. While we weren't exactly each other's chosen company, we had figured out how to enjoy ourselves as we rode out the storm. We had lots of good food and plenty to drink. I just hoped it wasn't a false calm before a storm of drunken tirades.

The lights flickered off and on as the wind howled outside. Then the power went off for good, and Mom lit the twin candelabras on the sideboard. The flickering candlelight cast long shadows but allowed us to see one another again.

Without electricity, we could have just as easily been sitting around a 19th-century candlelit dinner table instead of a 21st-century one. The flickering flames added to the atmosphere and even seemed to soften the petty rivalries around the table.

The dinner dishes had been cleared, and we all sat back in our chairs, content and stuffed from too much food. We sipped coffee and tea and nibbled on dessert. There was pumpkin pie with whipped cream, butter tarts, shortbread cookies and, of course, Mom's secret recipe Christmas cake.

Only Merlinda, Dominic, and Gail, our unsuspecting guests, had actually eaten the Christmas cake. I was thankful for the cake's somewhat delayed reaction. When our guests' stomachs protested later on, they would never suspect Mom's Christmas cake.

The rest of us stashed the cake in napkins, pockets, and purses for later disposal. In fact, the current power outage presented a great opportunity. I edged my dessert plate closer to the table edge and tipped it slightly until the cake fell into my palm. I wrapped it in my napkin and shoved it into my pocket.

"It's game time," Aunt Pearl announced. "This is going to be fun."

"No family games with guests here, Pearl," Mom said.

"Why not? I love games." Gail's expression brightened. "What are we playing?"

Aunt Amber clasped her hands together. "Ooh, let's play the Hungry Games!"

"Is that like *The Hunger Games*?" Gail asked.

"Yes and no," Aunt Amber said. "Instead of fighting for your area, you fight for food."

"But we already ate," Mom protested. "I'm too stuffed to even think about food, let alone fight for it."

"Me too," I said.

"You don't have to eat it, Ruby," Aunt Amber said. "We'll just use the food as a prop this time. Whoever wins the most food at the end will have their wish granted. Let's make it a game with a cargo cult theme!" She clapped her hands together.

In the West family, a wish meant a spell. I wondered how we would accommodate our non-witchy guests.

Mom laughed. "We'll use whatever dessert we have on the table. A fight to the death over my Christmas cake."

We all stared at her, open-mouthed.

After a few moments of awkward silence, Merlinda asked in a drunken slur, "What kind of game is that?"

"A dumb game," Aunt Pearl said. "I'm not motivated by food."

I agreed, though I didn't dare say so out loud. Using Mom's Christmas cake as poker chips was a recipe for disaster. The cake wouldn't be cleared off the table anytime soon, and our guests would be tempted to eat even more of the stuff. What if they got alcohol poisoning?

Suddenly, Merlinda leaned back in her chair, her eyelids drooping. The wine and booze-soaked Christmas cake had clearly affected her to the extent that she looked ready to pass out. The wine was all gone. Now we really had to get rid of the cake before she ate any more.

"I was only kidding about the cake fight." But Mom's crestfallen expression said otherwise. She had been deadly serious.

Aunt Amber sensed Mom's disappointment and quickly piped in. "Why don't we play truth or dare instead?"

"Great idea." In reality, I thought truth or dare was a terrible idea, given the assorted personalities around the table. But it beat eating or hiding more alcohol-soaked Christmas cake.

"I'll play as long as anything goes." Aunt Pearl smirked. "Winning at all costs is the name of the game."

"Count me in for that." Gail glared in Merlinda's direction. "I always come out on top."

I cast a warning glance at Aunt Pearl. "There are no winners in truth or dare. Just certain embarrassment and possible injury."

Mom sucked in her breath. "Nothing too reckless, though. We stop before anyone gets hurt."

"Don't change anything because of us," Gail said. "Just pretend you're having a normal family Christmas Eve."

Aunt Pearl smirked. "Hah! Our West family Christmas games are anything but normal. Be careful what you wish for."

I shuddered. We were witches after all, and our witchy games could get a little ugly because we were all so competitive. But sharing spells with outsiders, even other witches, was a definite no-no. Aunt Pearl's veiled threat worried me. Whatever schemes she had in mind for our guests would no doubt cross a line.

I knew that Aunt Pearl would never share details of our supernatural spells and secrets. But I still distrusted her. Maybe it was the Earl effect, or maybe she wanted to impress Merlinda with her spell casting. She normally disliked our family witch games, so her enthusiasm signaled danger. Something was percolating in that witchy mind of hers.

Of course, we all sprinkled a little witchcraft into our games. Normally, that wasn't a problem, but this time we were all in various stages of advanced inebriation. That included Aunt Pearl. Drunken spellcasting was dangerous without at least one sober witch to clean things up.

Aunt Pearl grinned sadistically. "Okay, listen up. Each couple is a team. Couple against couple. Everything's on the table."

Aunt Amber looked visibly relieved. "I guess Ruby and I are out then. We're the only ones without dates."

"Don't be silly," Aunt Pearl said. "You two are the sister act."

Mom shook her head. "No! I don't want to be—"

"Oh, c'mon, Ruby. It'll be fun." Aunt Amber brightened. "We'll win because we know each other so well."

"I doubt it," Dominic said. "Merlinda and I are gonna ace this thing. Right Merlinda?"

Merlinda's eyes fluttered open. She frowned. "Um, sure. I've never played truth or dare before, though."

"It's simple," I said. "One couple gets asked 'truth or dare'. If you choose truth, then you answer a question. Choose dare and you have to perform whatever is asked of you. Once you complete the task, you get to do the same to whoever you choose."

Grandma Vi floated behind Earl and Aunt Pearl. "Ooh! I can't wait to watch everybody self-destruct. I'll be the only one left standing."

Mom smiled.

Aunt Pearl pointed at Mom. "Ruby, you start."

"Okay, fine. Earl and Pearl…Truth or dare?"

"Truth." They both answered in unison, like an old married couple.

Mom giggled. "Why don't you tell us what you two did on your first date?"

"You can't ask that, Ruby!" Aunt Pearl's face flushed a deep crimson red.

"Why not? You said anything goes, Pearl." Mom raised her brows and smiled sweetly. "That goes for you too."

"We had a candlelight dinner at my place," Earl said. "It was very romantic, but I have to admit things got a little out of hand."

Aunt Amber snickered. "You two got hot and heavy? Oh my…I can see it now."

"Earl!" Aunt Pearl slapped his hand.

Earl recoiled. "It was hot all right. Especially after the curtains caught fire, and we had to call the fire department. Pearl loves her soy candles. You can melt them to make massage oil and…" He patted her hand. "I better not say any more. I'll never forget that night, though. Pearl's so full of surprises."

Tyler and I burst out laughing, followed by Mom. The thought of Aunt Pearl romancing anyone was beyond belief. Then again, Earl affected her in a way I had never seen before. She was under his spell, so to speak.

"Oh, Earl, stop. You're embarrassing me." Aunt Pearl turned toward Tyler and me and said rather abruptly, "Your turn. Truth or Dare?"

"Dare," Tyler said.

My heart skipped a beat, knowing that Aunt Pearl wanted nothing more than to ridicule Tyler. Dare was probably the wisest choice, though. I expected Aunt Pearl to have some embarrassing questions of her own.

"I dare you to leave town, sheriff." Aunt Pearl crossed her arms as she leaned back in her chair. "I'll even make it worth your while if you act quickly."

"That's not a valid dare, Pearl." Aunt Amber shook her head. "Next time make it something that can be done right here and now."

Tyler tossed his head back and laughed. "Nice try, Pearl. But even a bribe won't convince me to leave Westwick Corners anytime soon. I'm not leaving Cen, either."

"How much do you want? Whatever it is, I'll pay it."

"Pearl, stop it!" Mom wagged a finger at her older sister. "Tyler's not going anywhere, so get used to it."

Aunt Pearl's eyes narrowed. "If that's how you want to play it, fine. Don't ever say I didn't give you a way out, sheriff."

Tyler chuckled but didn't answer.

"You just wasted your turn, Aunt Pearl." At least she hadn't forced me to curse Tyler or cast some equally horrible spell.

Aunt Pearl scowled but remained silent. In her haste to deflect unwanted attention from herself and Earl, she had been too flustered to come up with a decent dare.

I turned to Brayden and Gail. "Truth or dare."

"Truth," Brayden smirked. "Ask me anything."

"You mean us," Gail corrected. "Ask us."

It was a perfect opportunity to learn more about their relationship. "What's the biggest secret you are keeping from your mate?" I asked. "Brayden, you go first."

Brayden flushed. "Well...um, Cen and I were once engaged."

Not what I was expecting. Apparently, not what Gail was expecting, either.

She bolted upright from her chair. "What? You brought me to your ex-girlfriend's house for dinner without telling me? You lied to me! You told me she was an old friend!"

"Well, she's both. I meant to say something...it just never came up in conversation, I guess." Brayden's eyes darted around the room looking for help.

Gail threw her hands in the air. "How would *that* naturally come up in conversation? I can't believe you didn't tell me, Brayden. You make me look like an idiot!"

We all looked away in awkward silence. No wonder Gail had thought nothing of coming for dinner. She had no clue that Brayden and I had almost married each other. I still didn't like her, but I did feel sorry for her right now.

Mom broke the silence. "Gail, your turn. What are you keeping from Brayden?"

"That I'm fed up with being ignored." She turned to Brayden. "I'm tired of you flirting with other women while I'm right here. You think I don't notice you ogling Merlinda? Everybody sees it. Right, Dominic?"

Merlinda's mouth dropped open in shock.

Dominic leaned away in his chair, clearly uncomfortable. "Uh… maybe we should move on. Who's next?"

"I'm not playing this stupid game anymore." Gail stood and threw her napkin down on the table. She marched into the kitchen.

Things had stayed rather civil until now, despite everyone's tipsy state. It was now clear that no matter what the game, Aunt Pearl had orchestrated everything to culminate in this exact moment where we were ready to bite each other's heads off.

Mom tilted her head toward the kitchen. "I think you should go after her, Brayden."

Brayden sighed and stood. "But why do I have to…oh, okay. But first…Dominic and Merlinda, truth or dare?"

"Truth," Dominic said. "Ask away."

"Do you think you'll ever get married?" Brayden didn't even hide it with Gail out of the room. He spoke to Dominic but gazed adoringly at Merlinda.

I glanced toward the kitchen door, hoping that Gail wasn't on the other side listening.

Dominic answered. "The answer's yes. Because we already are married."

CHAPTER 12

"What wedding?" Aunt Pearl choked on whatever she was eating. She looked visibly upset as she turned to Merlinda. "When did you get married? Why didn't you tell me?"

We were all too shocked to speak. Dominic's admission was the last thing any of us expected.

Merlinda's mouth dropped open. She glared at Dominic.

Aunt Pearl's eyes widened. "I can't believe you kept that from me, Merlinda. After everything I've done for you. I thought we shared everything."

"I would have told you eventually, Pearl. I just wasn't ready yet." Merlinda turned to Dominic. "You promised to keep it a secret."

"Yeah, but it's truth or dare, babe. And I just couldn't wait anymore. Nobody here knows your family, so what does it matter?"

I was at a loss for words. Aunt Pearl's revelation that she and Merlinda were confidantes was shocking, to say the least. And Dominic and Merlinda seemed such an odd match. He had to be at least a decade older than her, and his tough tattooed exterior was so at odds with Merlinda's refined fashion model looks.

"When did you get married?" Mom asked.

"Last semester break when Merlinda returned to Vanuatu." Dominic helped himself to a generous slice of Christmas cake and dropped it onto his plate. "We had a small private ceremony. Merlinda looked so beautiful in her dress."

The lights flickered several times before finally staying on again. I hoped they were on for good this time. Our drafty old mansion wasn't the coziest place to ride out a storm, and the darkness made it spooky.

Aunt Pearl turned to Merlinda. "You're barely old enough to get married. You'll ruin your life before it even starts."

Dominic glared at her. "Merlinda doesn't need advice from you, Pearl. She can make her own decisions."

"I'm twenty-one," Merlinda protested through a mouthful of Christmas cake. "I haven't dated much, but I really don't have to. I just know that Dominic's the one."

Dominic interjected. "You can't time true love. When love walks into your life, you grab it and don't let go."

I thought about grabbing the cake platter and taking it into the kitchen. Instead, I grabbed the last two pieces and put them on my plate. It was the only thing I could do to stop our guests from eating more.

Mom smiled. "I'm definitely making more next time."

"How could you not even invite me to your wedding?" Aunt Pearl's face flushed, angry at being excluded. Her disappointment was understandable, given the amount of time they spent together. Merlinda was basically her protégé and her only student at the moment. Then Dominic came along and spoiled everything. Even so, Aunt Pearl's anger bordered on unhealthy obsession.

"Nobody got invited," Dominic said. "We didn't want to make a fuss, so we had a secret wedding on Vanuatu. A couple of tourists were our witnesses, so absolutely no one knew. Until now. We just couldn't wait. Isn't that right, pumpkin?"

"Couldn't wait for what?" Gail emerged from the kitchen, frowning.

"Merlinda and Dominic secretly got married," Aunt Amber said. "And we only found out because of truth or dare."

Gail started to speak only to be interrupted by Merlinda.

"I—don't—feel—right." Merlinda dropped her fork and clutched her stomach. She pushed back her chair and staggered to her feet.

"What's wrong, dear?" Aunt Amber stood. She eyed Merlinda with concern.

Merlinda sat back down in her chair and closed her eyes. "I'll be okay, just give me a minute."

Her rapid breathing and flushed skin said otherwise.

"Maybe you should lie down. Let me help you to the sofa." I stood just as the lights went off again.

The room was dark except for the dim candlelight and Grandma Vi's softly glowing apparition as she floated above the sideboard like an oversized nightlight. Her soft glow illuminated the dining room just enough to see Merlinda hunched over across the table, wincing in pain.

Aunt Pearl noticed it too. "Geez, Merlinda…you don't look so hot."

"My stomach is really upset. Excuse me." Merlinda rose from the table and staggered to the dining room doorway. She paused a moment to steady herself. Then she disappeared into the darkness of the living room.

Dominic jumped to his feet. "I'd better go help her."

Aunt Pearl stepped in front of Dominic and waved him away. "No, I'll help her."

I wasn't surprised that Merlinda was sick given how much alcohol-laden Christmas cake she had eaten. I only wished I could have stopped her without Mom knowing.

All conversation ceased as we listened to Merlinda stumble through the living room and into the hallway toward the bathroom.

Outside the wind howled, the gusts rattling the ancient single-paned windows.

The lights flickered again and turned back on for about thirty seconds. Then the power went out again. Seconds later a draft blew out all the candles. We sat in darkness and said nothing. We were all transfixed by Merlinda's agonized retching in the hallway.

Merlinda hadn't made it as far as the bathroom yet. She repeatedly refused all offers of help, but it was killing me to sit still and do nothing.

"I'll get some more matches." I rose from my seat and felt my way along the seat backs toward the kitchen door. My eyes slowly adjusted to the darkness, and after what seemed like an eternity, I finally navigated through the kitchen to the built-in desk where we kept matches. I rummaged through drawer after drawer, frantically searching for matches before finding some in a bottom drawer.

I lit the candle on the kitchen counter and carried it out into the dining room. After relighting both candelabras on the sideboard I set my candle down on the table, relieved to see familiar faces once more.

I had just sat down when Merlinda screamed.

CHAPTER 13

We all jumped from our seats and raced to the doorway. Dominic and Brayden collided by the sideboard, almost knocking over the candelabras.

Dominic swore under his breath and grabbed a candelabra. He brandished it like a weapon and forced Brayden out of the way.

I shrunk against the wall and let both of them pass. Given Brayden's obsession with Merlinda and his need to always be first, I didn't want to get in his way. I motioned for Tyler to go ahead of me too. Then I picked up the second candelabra and followed the men out into the hallway.

I almost ran into Tyler's backside as he stopped abruptly in front of me.

Aunt Amber swore as she slammed to a halt behind me. "What the heck is going on?"

"Merlinda!" Dominic's wail sent a chill up my spine.

No answer.

I craned my neck to see around Tyler and saw Merlinda lying on the floor. Dominic knelt beside her. His lit candelabra sat on the hall table and illuminated the otherwise dark hallway. The flickering light only intensified the dark mood.

Merlinda was curled in a fetal position in the hallway, unconscious. She had collapsed before reaching the bathroom.

"Merlinda! Talk to me." Dominic shook Merlinda's shoulder, his voice breaking. "Wake up!"

Tyler walked around Merlinda and knelt on her opposite side. He lifted her arm, but it was limp. He leaned over her and checked for a pulse and vital signs. "She's not breathing."

I followed Tyler and stood behind him. I placed my candelabra on the floor by the wall.

"Somebody call an ambulance, quick!" Tyler turned sideways and began CPR. His broad torso partially blocked my view, but even so, it was painfully obvious that the CPR wasn't yielding results.

"I already did." Westwick Corners was so small we didn't actually have 9-1-1. Or, unfortunately, a hospital or paramedics. Even the closest doctor was an hour away in Shady Creek. I had called Shady Creek Emergency anyway, hoping for a miracle. But the storm was so fierce that even the paramedics were grounded. "Unfortunately, they can't get here in the storm."

A minute passed, then a few more. Even in the dim light, Merlinda's bluish skin tone was evident. It didn't look good.

Tyler and Dominic took turns performing CPR, though it soon became obvious to us all that his efforts were futile.

Finally, Tyler stood and turned to Dominic. "I'm so sorry, Dominic. We did everything we could, but...she's gone."

"She's not gone. She can't be. She just fainted. We have to keep trying." Dominic shoved Tyler out of the way and resumed CPR, though it was obvious from his technique that he had never resuscitated anyone before.

"Dominic, I'm so sorry." Brayden placed a hand on Dominic's shoulder.

Dominic brushed Brayden's hand away. "She's not gone. She's just..."

Aunt Pearl shoved in front of Brayden and knelt beside Merlinda. "Let me see her. I'll get her to the hospital."

Tyler's eyes met mine. Clearly, he thought the same thing I did. Not even magic would bring Merlinda back to life.

Aunt Pearl rose to her feet and stood completely still as the gravity of the situation hit her.

"What the hell is happening? Just a few minutes ago she was..." Dominic shook his head in disbelief. He slowly backed away from Merlinda and leaned against the wall, defeated. He slumped down into a sitting position and covered his face with his hands. His whole body shook as he cried into his hands. "She can't die on me."

Dominic was clearly distraught at losing his sweetheart.

He wasn't the only one.

Aunt Pearl screamed. "No!" She collapsed on the floor beside Merlinda and curled up into a fetal position.

The rest of us stood frozen in place, stunned. An apparently healthy twenty-something woman had passed away right in front of our eyes with no logical explanation.

Merlinda's hands clutched her stomach in a death grip, her face frozen in a grimace. Her eyes remained wide open, unseeing. Even in the dim candlelight, it was obvious she was dead.

"I'm sorry, Pearl." Tyler gently pulled Aunt Pearl up into a standing position and placed his arm around her shoulders. He steered her toward Aunt Amber and Mom, who both sobbed quietly a few feet away.

Dominic sobbed into his hands. "She was eating and talking and everything was fine. I don't understand what happened. How can someone so young just die like that?"

Tyler shook his head. "Sometimes people die suddenly. Maybe she had an undiagnosed medical condition. We'll have to wait and see what the medical examiner says."

The medical examiner, like pretty much everyone else, was in Shady Creek.

Mom's hand flew to her mouth in shock. "I can't believe it. She was the picture of health. She had such a healthy appetite too. She was just enjoying my Christmas cake."

Aunt Pearl jumped to her feet and shook her fist at Mom. "You have to stop making that cake, Ruby. Your stupid cake killed my star student."

"You think I poisoned Merlinda?" Mom's mouth dropped open, aghast at Aunt Pearl's accusation. "That's crazy. What about everyone else? You all ate the cake and you're not sick."

Actually, only Merlinda, Gail, and Dominic had sampled the cake. The rest of us had stashed our cake, uneaten. But Mom didn't know that. I patted her shoulder, relieved that so far Gail and Dominic showed no symptoms. Yet. "Aunt Pearl didn't mean—"

"Damn right, I meant it, Cendrine. It's Ruby's fault that Merlinda's dead." Aunt Pearl paced back and forth, clearly distraught. "I'll never have another student like Merlinda. All that talent, destroyed by a few crumbs of poison cake."

Mom sucked in her breath. "It can't be my cake, Pearl. It's the same recipe I make every year. How can there be anything wrong with it?"

"Uh…Ruby, there's something I need to ask about." Earl shifted uncomfortably on his feet. "You know how I was helping you with that rat problem?"

Gail sucked in her breath. "You have rats in this place?"

"Afraid so," Earl said. "Thing is, I set the measuring cup of rat poison on the counter for a minute, and when I went back for it a couple of minutes later, it was gone."

Mom gasped. "You don't think that…you mean the white powder in my measuring cup wasn't flour? I used it in the cake."

"If you didn't fill the measuring cup yourself, then why did you use it, Ruby?" Tyler asked. "How did you even know it was flour?"

Tears ran down Mom's cheeks. "I-I wasn't thinking, I guess. I thought it was weird because I didn't remember using that measuring cup. But I've been run off my feet lately and just thought I had measured it out earlier and forgotten all about it. I've been so busy organizing the dinner with all of Pearl's last-minute guests that I lost track of things."

I scowled at Aunt Pearl's insult to Mom's cake and, indirectly, my Pearl's Charm School dropout status. "Even if Merlinda was poisoned, it could be from anything. Like your herbal tea, for instance."

"Hey, I ate that cake and there's nothing wrong with me," Dominic said. "It can't be the cake."

"You probably weigh twice as much as Merlinda," Brayden pointed out. "You can absorb the poison better. Either that, or it just takes longer to affect you."

Dominic's hand flew to his mouth. "I don't feel so hot all of a sudden."

Gail nodded. "I ate some too, and I'm not sick. You sure it was rat poison? I feel just fine."

'Some' was a bit of an understatement. Gail had probably eaten four or five pieces by my count. Yet she showed no signs of poisoning.

Aunt Pearl pulled her hand from her pocket and gave me the finger. As she did, a crumpled piece of paper fell to the floor.

"Such a tragedy." Aunt Amber stooped to pick up the paper. She frowned as she unrolled it and read the writing. "Uh-oh. Your milk thistle tea remedy has a mistake, Pearl. Instead of milk thistle, it says mistletoe. You know mistletoe is poisonous, right?"

"Of course I know—let me see that." Aunt Pearl snatched the paper from Aunt Amber's hand.

Aunt Amber shook her head as she stared at Merlinda's lifeless body. "Oh my god, Pearl. What have you done?"

CHAPTER 14

"You killed Merlinda," Dominic screamed. "She was finally going home and leaving you for good. You knew you couldn't keep her trapped here at your stupid school forever. So you poisoned her tea and killed her."

"Pearl didn't do it on purpose. It was an accident." Mom's words hung in the air as we all fell silent.

Dominic lunged toward Aunt Pearl. "I'm going to kill you, old lady."

Brayden and Tyler intercepted Dominic just as he reached Aunt Pearl. Each grabbed a shoulder and restrained him, but just barely.

I had no idea what Dominic meant about Aunt Pearl keeping Merlinda in Westwick Corners, but there was probably some basis in truth. Aunt Pearl sometimes resorted to drastic measures when she didn't get her way. But killing Merlinda to prevent her from leaving? No way. I couldn't imagine her doing that.

It was the kind of stuff you heard on Dateline. People got desperate when love was at stake. And even though Aunt Pearl's relationship with Merlinda was more of a mentor and protégé arrangement, Aunt Pearl was very attached to her. In fact, she was obsessed with her. If Merlinda had really planned to leave Pearl's Charm School for good, then I didn't doubt that Aunt Pearl would mete out her own brand of vigilante justice.

As a former student, I knew that first-hand.

But kill Merlinda? Never.

"Don't be ridiculous." Aunt Pearl smirked, her voice suddenly calm. "I'm a reasonable person, and I would never stand in Merlinda's way. It wasn't me she wanted to leave, you know."

Tyler's eyes narrowed. "What are you implying, Pearl?"

Aunt Pearl rolled her eyes. "Figure it out yourself, sheriff. Do your job."

"Aunt Pearl, answer Tyler's question." Her flippant answer struck me as really odd. A minute ago she had been hysterical.

"I didn't kill anyone." Aunt Pearl shook a fist at Dominic. "Why on earth would I poison my own student? Dead students aren't exactly a testimonial for Pearl's Charm School, now are they? How could I attract new students?"

I wondered that myself but hadn't dared to ask. As far as I knew, Aunt Pearl didn't advertise or even have a website. Everything was word of mouth, which was how Merlinda had found Pearl's Charm School in the first place. She'd traveled halfway around the world to attend, only to suffer such a sad fate.

Dominic struggled to break free from Tyler and Brayden, but they held him firmly by the arms. "I'll tell you why you killed her. Because she was better than you. Merlinda told me you were jealous of her talent. You didn't want her out in the world upstaging you because then everyone would know that she was better than you. Admit it."

At least he hadn't added that Aunt Pearl was better *as a witch*. Brayden knew about our witchy talents—sort of. He dismissed us as new age nutcases, not witches. He figured that our herbs, talismans, and potions were just a bunch of strange family hobbies and was oblivious to whatever went on right under his nose. He had no idea about all the stuff Aunt Pearl pulled on him enchantment-wise, purely for her own personal amusement.

Tyler, on the other hand, knew about our supernatural secrets. Aside from Brayden's willful blindness, it was really only Gail who had no clue that we were witches.

And it had to stay that way.

Aunt Pearl snorted. "Jealous? Why would I be jealous? I taught Merlinda everything she knew."

"Now Pearl, take it easy on Dominic. He just lost Merlinda." Mom placed an arm around Aunt Pearl and steered her out of the hallway and into the living room. Aunt Amber and I followed.

Mom and Aunt Amber collapsed onto the sofa, one on each side of Aunt Pearl like sisterly prison guards. I stood by the doorway, ready to block Aunt Pearl in case she made a run at Dominic.

"Well, I just lost my protégé. Doesn't anyone care how I feel?" Aunt Pearl flushed with anger as she wrested her arm away from Aunt Amber. "What kind of teacher poisons her own students? Certainly not me."

Aunt Amber held up her hand. "I'm not saying you poisoned her on purpose, Pearl. You just got a little sloppy and wrote the spell down wrong. We all make mistakes sometimes. You know, milk thistle, mistletoe…easy to mix up."

Aunt Pearl scowled. "Maybe you're sloppy or confused, Amber. Not me. I'm much too sharp to make a mistake like that. How can you even suggest such a thing? We have a killer in our midst."

"We don't know that's the case," I said. "Merlinda's death sure seems suspicious, but only the medical examiner can determine the cause of death. All we can do is preserve the evidence."

"Evidence?" Mom shuddered. "I don't like where this is going."

"Cen's right," Aunt Amber said. "With the storm outside it will be awhile before the medical examiner gets here, so we have to make sure everything is left exactly as it is."

We had to at least convince Aunt Pearl to keep her hands—and witchcraft—to herself. Covering up a mistake could have dire consequences.

"You honestly think I poisoned her?" Aunt Pearl searched our faces for answers. "I think someone is trying to frame me. I'll bet it's that damn Sheriff Gates."

"Don't be ridiculous, Aunt Pearl," I said. "He had nothing to do with Merlinda's death. He hasn't been anywhere near her." Tyler had arrived late and sat beside me on the opposite side of the table. He had never been out of my sight.

Aunt Amber and Mom exchanged worried glances. I knew what they were thinking. We had to do something before Aunt Pearl took drastic action.

Whether it was an accident or a calculated crime, Aunt Pearl was an unlikely suspect on either count. She was a perfectionist and hardly ever made mistakes. She rarely made mistakes with her spells, certainly not with a simple tea concoction.

On the other hand, we had all eaten the same dinner, but only Merlinda had ingested Aunt Pearl's tea.

However, Aunt Pearl had a lot to lose from even a simple mistake. Her school's reputation, for one. As if she read my mind, Aunt Pearl said, "This was no accident. And there was nothing wrong with my tea."

Aunt Amber tapped on the paper with a manicured nail. "But the recipe says mistletoe right here—"

Aunt Pearl grabbed the recipe from Aunt Amber. "Just stop it, Amber! I purposely wrote it down wrong as a safeguard so no one could steal my recipe."

"Admit you're wrong, Pearl." Aunt Amber tried to grab the paper back, but Aunt Pearl ripped it up into tiny pieces.

Aunt Amber rolled her eyes. "Now you're destroying evidence. Not that it helps you any. Your tea will be tested."

"Oh, this is ridiculous! I would never make a mistake like that. I'll prove it." Aunt Pearl grabbed Merlinda's teacup from the coffee table and gulped down whatever remained in the teacup. The teacup rattled as she dropped it onto the saucer. "See. Perfectly harmless."

I gasped. "You just drank the evidence."

"And poisoned yourself in the process, dummy," Aunt Amber

added. "I hope we'll be able to save you in time, since this type of poison isn't instantaneous. How long ago did Melinda drink the tea?"

"Oh, I don't know." Aunt Pearl turned to me. "When Cen was in the snow globe. Maybe a couple of hours ago? How long does it take to poison someone?"

CHAPTER 15

We stepped back into the hallway to see what the men were doing. It was hard to move around with everyone jostling for position. Dominic knelt beside Merlinda, and Tyler crouched on her opposite side. The rest of us crowded around them.

I scanned the hall and noticed that someone was missing. "Where's Earl?"

"I thought he was in the living room with you guys," Brayden said.

"No." Normally Earl never left Aunt Pearl's side. I flashed back to the rat poison and figured he had returned to the kitchen to double check Mom's measuring cup. But the rat poison didn't explain why only Merlinda was affected. She wasn't the only one who had eaten the Christmas cake. Maybe Merlinda's reaction wasn't from the cake at all.

Tyler's eyes met mine. "Cen, make sure nobody touches anything. I've got to make a call."

I nodded and watched Tyler exit into the living room. Easier said than done.

Aunt Amber pushed past Mom and me and tapped Dominic's

shoulder. "Get out of the way and let me have a look. I can tell instantly if Merlinda was poisoned by mistletoe."

Dominic dismissed her with a wave of a hand. "Don't you dare touch her. You're not a doctor. We'll have to wait till he gets here."

Uh-oh.

"You just assume that the medical examiner is a man?" Aunt Amber asked. "In fact, the ME is a woman. Why would you assume otherwise?"

"Because duh, medical examiner. Of course he's a man. Women don't do well at that sort of thing," Dominic said.

"What you really mean is that you don't like women doing well at all, do you, Dominic?" Aunt Amber's eyes narrowed. "You sure didn't like Merlinda outshining you. You can't face the fact that I'm an expert in my field, either. Even if that means getting to the bottom of what happened to your wife."

Aunt Amber was a feminist, herbalist, and witch in that order. She was also a force to be reckoned with on those rare occasions when she lost her temper. This was one of those times.

Dominic stood to challenge Aunt Amber. He just had to get the last word in. "I like women in their place—cooking and cleaning. Except of course, when the cooking doesn't go too well."

"You're skating on thin ice, sonny," Aunt Pearl warned. "There's nothing wrong with Ruby's cooking."

"Wait a minute—" Mom stepped forward, but it was too late.

"Hey! What the hell—" Dominic braced against Aunt Amber as she pushed him away from Merlinda's body and tossed him toward the living room doorway with one hand. He stumbled backward before he crashed through the doorway and collapsed in a heap just inside the living room.

Judging by Dominic's puzzled expression, he was clearly mystified at how tiny Aunt Amber had just out-muscled him. "How did you just do that?"

"Wouldn't you like to know?" Aunt Amber didn't wait for an answer. "I happen to be very good at my job."

She brushed her palms together as if wiping them clean of Dominic. Her job of dispensing justice to Dominic completed, she knelt beside Merlinda. She studied Melinda's face, careful not to touch her. She leaned in and inhaled the air near Merlinda's mouth.

Mom stood between Dominic and Aunt Amber, ready to act. She had powers to stop Dominic, even though she was reluctant to use them. That was obvious from her deer-in-the-headlights expression.

"You should have seen that coming, Dominic." Aunt Pearl's eyes narrowed. "Now I see what Merlinda was talking about."

"You're bluffing. Merlinda never said anything to you about me." Dominic looked scared. "Did she?"

Aunt Pearl placed a finger to her mouth. "My lips are sealed. I never betray a confidence. Merlinda told me everything you were up to, so don't try anything smart."

Dominic reddened. He opened his mouth but reconsidered. He clamped his mouth shut without saying another word.

Aunt Amber looked up, her face tinged with worry. "Merlinda was definitely poisoned."

Tyler finished his call and dropped his cell phone into his pocket as he stepped back into the hall. "Okay, everybody out and into the living room. Except you, Brayden. We'll move Merlinda into the study and lock the door until the ME gets here."

Brayden nodded, though he looked queasy and very reluctant to touch a now lifeless Merlinda.

Dominic protested but was quickly shut down by Brayden in his usual blunt and abrasive manner. "Tyler is right, Dominic. We can't leave Melinda here on the floor in the hallway. We have to move her."

Grandma Vi hovered beside Brayden. Of course only us witches could hear her, but she said it anyway. "Any witch worth their salt can get into a locked room. There's quite a few of us here."

That's exactly what I was afraid of.

CHAPTER 16

I followed Mom, Gail, and the others into the living room while Dominic sat with his back against the wall just inside the living room doorway. He hadn't even bothered to get up, afraid that Aunt Amber would assault him again. His gaze flitted back and forth between Aunt Amber in the living room and Tyler and Brayden in the hallway. The two men were still strategizing on how best to move Merlinda's lifeless body into the study.

I felt sorry for Dominic on some level, but he made me suspicious too. Not just because his surprise visit to Westwick Corners coincided with his new—and young—wife's sudden death. The secret wedding was also a red flag. Maybe he stood to gain, financially or otherwise, from Merlinda's death. Whatever the circumstances, Dominic had plenty of explaining to do.

I was certain that Dominic's grief was genuine. He turned and peered over his shoulder into the hallway. Within seconds he burst into tears. His whole body shook as he sobbed uncontrollably.

"Somebody make him stop." Grandma Vi hovered. "I feel like I'm in a really bad soap opera."

"I can't believe all this is happening to me. I should have just stayed home." Gail perched on the arm of my overstuffed chair even though there was plenty of space on the loveseat and sofa.

I wished she had stayed home too, but saying so would just infuriate her.

Gail's comment was awfully selfish and self-absorbed given that someone had just died. Brayden had somehow managed to find a partner who was just as self-centered as he was. On the other hand, Gail had probably never expected to spend Christmas Eve with her boyfriend at his ex-fiancé's house.

I wondered what Gail thought of my crazy family. And me. Brayden had probably told her we were all nuts. Why did I even care what Gail thought in the first place? On some level I wanted Gail to regret ever accepting Aunt Pearl's suspicious last-minute invitation. But self-centered or not, she hadn't created the situation she found herself in.

I glanced beside me, shocked at what I saw. While the rest of us sat in stunned silence, Gail rummaged through her giant purse. She alternated between filing her nails and checking her phone for messages. Apparently, even sudden death wasn't enough to hold her attention.

The combined light from Gail's phone and the candelabra cast a strange glow and accentuated the shadows on the living room walls, adding to the already eerie vibe.

Aunt Pearl broke the silence. "Why do I always get blamed for everything? I guarantee you there was nothing wrong with my tea. Believe me, when I poison someone, it happens quickly. Just like that." She snapped her fingers for effect.

"What do you mean, *when* you poison someone?" Aunt Amber's mouth dropped open. "You've done this before?"

As a WICCA executive, Aunt Amber was required to report any witchy wrongdoings, something Aunt Pearl was well aware of. Aunt Pearl was playing a dangerous game, one where we could all bear the brunt of her reckless claims.

"She didn't mean..." Mom's voice trailed off as the gravity of Aunt Pearl's words sank in.

"Of course I meant it," Aunt Pearl snapped. "I'm not getting into specifics, but let's just say if you cross me, you'll regret it big-time."

Aunt Pearl was still in complete denial about everything from Merlinda's sudden death to the possibility that a mistake in her tea remedy had something to do with it. Yet she now insinuated that she would kill anyone who crossed her.

"You're lying. You wouldn't purposely poison someone." I glanced into the hallway. Brayden stood guard by Merlinda, but Tyler was nowhere in sight. Just as well. Aunt Pearl's incriminating poison comments would just compel him to investigate and possibly sidetrack things.

"That depends."

I sighed. "I don't know why you're trying to distract us from the tragedy of what's happened. Face it, Aunt Pearl. You made a mistake. We all make mistakes sometimes. It's better for everyone if you just own up to it."

Aunt Pearl stood and folded her scrawny arms across her chest. "I refuse to answer on the grounds that it might incriminate me. I'm not divulging my secrets. That includes my secret tea recipe. About the poison...you guys have nothing to worry about."

"What secret recipe?" Aunt Amber tapped her finger on a piece of paper. "I've got another copy of your recipe right here. I found it lying on the kitchen counter."

"What? No, you don't." Aunt Pearl pulled a folded paper out of her bra. She sighed, visibly relieved. "That's just another decoy recipe. I always alter the ingredients just in case the recipe falls into enemy hands." She snatched the paper from Aunt Amber.

"Oh, for crying out loud, Pearl, just own up. You made a mistake." Aunt Amber pointed to the hall. "Please just admit it before Tyler goes off on a tangent thinking someone was murdered. And don't go telling anyone else that you're in the habit of poisoning people on purpose."

"I did not poison Merlinda. I keep telling you, my tea was perfectly fine. I drank it myself, and look at me. I'm perfff-ectly fine." Her voice trembled as she spoke.

"No, you're not. Your teeth are chattering." Aunt Amber frowned. "I don't know why you're trying to sidetrack things, but it's disrespectful to Merlinda to say the least. Don't you want the sheriff to get to the bottom of this? Now he thinks her death is suspicious. You're turning a tragic accident into a murder investigation."

"I'm doing no such thing," Aunt Pearl snapped. "Sheriff Gates couldn't find a killer on death row in a super-max prison. Stop blaming me and focus on finding Merlinda's real killer. We all know the sheriff never will."

"Don't talk about Tyler that way," I whispered. "And lower your voice. I won't be part of whatever conspiracy you're cooking up."

"Cen's right, Pearl," Mom said. "Tyler is a wonderful sheriff. You don't want to get on his bad side. Just admit your mistake."

"Oh, for crying out loud, Ruby. There's nothing wrong with my tea. Sheriff Gates is out to frame me. Maybe he killed Merlinda."

I walked over to Aunt Pearl and held the candelabra up to her face. She looked pale and a thin sheen of sweat coated her forehead. Her dilated pupils were visible even in the dim light.

I doubted that the candlelight was enough to dilate a seventy-year-old's pupils, yet Aunt Pearl's were noticeably enlarged. Maybe it was due to all the excitement and shock at Merlinda's death. Or maybe her eyes had reacted to something worse, like poison.

I stepped closer. "Are you sure you're okay, Aunt Pearl? You don't look so hot."

Aunt Pearl raised her hand, shielding her eyes. "For crying out loud, Cen, get that light out of my face. And stop bombarding me with questions. This interrogation is uncalled for. What's next—waterboarding?"

I opened my mouth but thought better of it. At least she remained her usual cantankerous self. That was a good sign, and I didn't want to antagonize her further. But she looked awfully unsteady. I placed the candelabra on the coffee table. "Mom, come help me."

"Ooh…I feel tired all of a sudden. I really need to sit down." Aunt Pearl's hand trembled as she touched her forehead.

Mom and I steered Aunt Pearl to the sofa, and not a moment too soon.

Aunt Pearl's legs buckled under, and she collapsed onto the sofa. She clutched her stomach and slowly slid down into a lying position. "I don't feel so hot."

The room suddenly brightened, but it wasn't the electricity coming back on.

It was Merlinda's doing. Though she was gone, her tropical snow globe still glowed. It waxed and waned, casting an eerie light throughout the darkened living room. She was—or had been—such a powerful witch that the residue of her powers remained even after her death.

Which was weird. Creepy, in fact. It was a testament to Merlinda's supernatural powers. Yet, despite her strength, someone had still gotten the better of her.

"Cen?" Aunt Pearl sat up and croaked in a raspy voice. "How long does it take to poison someone? You're an expert in these sorts of things."

I couldn't answer even if I wanted to. I was rendered speechless, intoxicated by Merlinda's globe as it grew brighter. Now it pulsated with light and seemed to take on a life of its own. It was beautiful.

My jealousy toward Merlinda seemed so petty now. All these months, I could have reached out and befriended her. She had been alone in a strange country, away from family and friends. And I had purposely shunned her when I could have protected her. It was too late for any of that now, and I regretted my pettiness.

"I don't know anything about poisoning people." I glared at Aunt Pearl. "Don't you dare try to shift the blame onto me."

"Oh Cen, relax." Aunt Pearl let out a heavy sigh. "Everybody knows that you're a lousy witch and couldn't even poison a flea if your life depended on it. I just thought that with your journalist background that you would know something about poisons in general. I was testing your knowledge. Just so you know, you failed miserably."

Aunt Pearl seemed to have completely recovered from whatever calamity had struck her moments ago. Maybe it was all an act.

"Let's refocus on Merlinda." I turned to Aunt Amber. "Can't you make her cooperate?"

Aunt Amber shrugged as if to absolve herself of any responsibility for her sister. She obviously feared provoking Aunt Pearl further. She pointed at the empty teacup. "Kind of late for that."

"You're overreacting as usual, Cen," Aunt Pearl brightened. "I'll just do a rewind spell. Merlinda will come back, none of us will eat or drink anything more, and everything will be fine."

"Don't be ridiculous," Aunt Amber said. "You can't do rewind spells on yourself."

"Fine, Amber. You think you know everything, so you do it." Aunt Pearl glared at Aunt Amber and held her arms up in surrender. "Rewind me."

I glanced out to the hallway just as Tyler reappeared in the door-way. He and Brayden had moved Merlinda during our heated discussion. Brayden was nowhere to be seen though.

Tyler sidestepped Dominic as he entered the living room. "Nobody's rewinding anything."

Aunt Amber sniffed. "He's right, Pearl. We don't want to cover up the accident."

"I keep telling you—it was no accident!" Aunt Pearl shot up from the sofa, all signs of illness gone. "You're not listening to me!"

Dominic frowned. He stood and left the living room for the hall.

Earl still hadn't reappeared, and I wondered what he was doing. Tyler had instructed all of us to stay in the living room, but that was after Earl had vanished.

Brayden no longer stood in the hall either, but I figured he'd lie low after being forced to assist Tyler. On the other hand, it was strange that he wasn't sitting on the sofa with Gail trying to make me jealous or something.

Aunt Amber frowned. "One more thing, Pearl. If Merlinda was murdered as you claim, how could you even rewind the spell in the first place? You wouldn't know enough details to rewind. Is there something you're not telling us?"

Gail looked up from filing her nails. "What on earth are you people talking about?"

We all ignored her.

Aunt Pearl stomped her foot and scowled. "Stop changing the subject, Amber. I keep telling you, I am absolutely certain that there was nothing wrong with my tea. It's murder."

"I'll be the judge of that." Tyler picked up the teacup with a gloved hand and deposited it into a plastic bag.

"Arrest me and you'll pay, Sheriff Gates."

Tyler rolled his eyes. "You just never know when to quit, Pearl."

Aunt Pearl waved a bony arm in the air. "Why don't you quit this town, Sheriff Gates? We don't need you here."

He winked at Aunt Pearl. "I think that you really do need me. I keep you out of trouble."

"Nobody keeps me out of anything. Especially not you, Sheriff!! I'm into plenty you don't know about. Don't give yourself credit you don't deserve."

"Aunt Pearl, stop arguing—" I was interrupted by Earl.

"I found my measuring cup." Earl stood in the dining room doorway, his face flushed and sweating. His Santa suit was half unbuttoned, revealing a plaid work shirt underneath. Both his shirt and the suit were covered in a dusting of white powder. "It was almost the same as Ruby's, but the one I used for the poison had a cracked spout."

"Oh no! That is the measuring cup I used. I remember it now." Mom jumped up from the sofa and screamed as she ran into the dining room.

My heart thumped in my chest as I ran after Mom.

I stared at the dining room table. The Christmas cake platter was empty. Not a crumb remained, but there was something else in its place.

Two dead mice.

"Oh my god!" Mom screamed. "We're all going to die!"

CHAPTER 17

I placed my arm around Mom and squeezed her shoulder to console her. "Maybe the mice were already poisoned from Earl's concoction before they hopped onto the table." I turned to Earl and asked the obvious. "Were they already on the plate, or did you put them there?"

"Of course I didn't put them there. Why would I do that?" Earl wiped his sweaty brow. "I went to change out of this stupid Santa suit—it's so damn hot—and that's when I saw the dead mice on the table."

"How did you get that flour all over you?" Aunt Amber's eyes narrowed as she looked suspiciously at Earl. A dusting of white powder covered the top half of his Santa suit. "Mistaking it for rat poison again?"

Earl shook his head and held out his hands in protest. "No…that's not what happened at all. But I had to know whether or not Ruby got my measuring cup mixed up with hers. It's been driving me nuts, and I couldn't live with myself if that happened, so I went back into the kitchen to test it."

"How exactly do you do a toxicology test on an empty measuring cup?" Aunt Amber asked.

"I never said it was scientific or anything." Earl looked down at his oversized Santa belt buckle. "But if it was my rat poison, there is a way to tell."

"How?" I asked.

"I filled the empty measuring cup with water. It didn't fizz, so that told me that it really was just flour in Ruby's measuring cup." He frowned as he saw we weren't following his logic. "My homemade rat poison recipe fizzes if you add water."

"You make your own poison?" I shuddered, thinking that home-made poison sounded like something Aunt Pearl would do. Maybe they weren't so different from each other after all. I wondered how many more deadly recipes were in our house.

Earl rolled his eyes. "Of course I make my own. I'm a farmer so I improvise. I used flour, sugar, baking soda, and a little peanut butter. Oh…and a small amount of warfarin."

I frowned. "The blood thinner?"

Earl nodded. "Just a small dose is toxic to rodents. The amount I used is harmless to humans, just like the rest of the ingredients. The peanut butter, flour, and sugar attract the critters, and then the baking soda and warfarin kills them by giving them both gas and ulcers. People can fart but mice and rats can't. All that gas is fatal to them. The warfarin is just an extra measure. Works like magic." Earl snapped his fingers for effect.

"So my cake wasn't poisonous after all?"

Earl shook his head. "Not unless you're a rodent who can't pass gas."

Mom pressed her palms together in a prayer gesture. "Thank goodness I didn't kill anyone."

I shrugged. "I guess we're right back to square one."

Aunt Pearl gave me a blank stare.

"Your tea." I was only half-joking because Aunt Pearl's bruised ego often led to drastic actions. Judging by the cargo cult accounts and my own first-hand experience with the snow globe, Merlinda was already a better witch than Aunt Pearl. After all, Merlinda had single-hand-edly fooled an entire South Pacific island nation with her witchcraft. A tall order even for the most expert of witches.

I glanced at her snow globe. It seemed to glow even brighter than it had just moments ago.

"Thanks for nothing, Earl." Aunt Pearl scowled. "I really thought we had something special together."

"Of course we do, Pearl," Earl said. "But we all make mistakes now and then. I make plenty, which is why I double-checked to be sure I hadn't messed up the ingredients in my own recipe and possibly cont-aminated Ruby's by using the same measuring cup. I even tested it myself to be sure. Anybody can make a mistake. If you think you acci-dentally poisoned Merlinda, then you should just say so."

Mom nodded. "I know it's hard to admit mistakes, but we all make them. Even my perfectionist sister."

Aunt Pearl dropped her head into her hands. "I-I just don't know anymore. I'm always so careful, but with all the stuff going on, maybe I did mix up a few ingredients."

Aunt Pearl was such a stickler for detail. It was hard to imagine that she had made a mistake, even with her admission. Milk thistle and mistletoe differed dramatically in appearance, for one. Any change in her tea ingredients had to be deliberate, not accidental.

On the other hand, she was love struck and had been increasingly absent-minded about other things lately. She was also getting older. Maybe forgetfulness was inevitable. I flashed back to my snow globe fiasco. Aunt Pearl could be mean-spirited, but she would never leave me outside in the frigid cold to freeze to death. Especially not in front of other people. No, Aunt Pearl's justice was always meted out in private.

Had she taken things a little too far with Merlinda? Most teachers took joy in their students' achievements, even when they eclipsed their teacher. But Aunt Pearl would be crushed if Merlinda had outshone her with witchcraft. Would she stand for that?

In a word, no.

I shifted my gaze to Merlinda's tropical snow globe. Against all odds, the globe grew even brighter and now pulsated with energy. That was some powerful magic.

CHAPTER 18

I tore my gaze from Merlinda's snow globe and refocused on Aunt Pearl. Aunt Amber's constant mention of the mistletoe tea was irritating, but Aunt Pearl needed to own up to her mistakes.

Her tea couldn't be ruled out until it was tested for toxins and eliminated from consideration. I suspected she had accidentally added mistletoe instead of milk thistle. Deep down I wanted Aunt Pearl to realize that no one is perfect. Not even her.

Drawing the wrong conclusions about Aunt Pearl's tea, Mom's cake, or anything else for that matter, could lead the investigation in the wrong direction, though. It was time to set matters straight.

Dominic appeared in the living room doorway, boots on and jacket in hand.

Aunt Amber gasped. "You can't leave."

"You can't force me to stay here. Somebody just killed my wife, and the sheriff's not doing anything about it. He won't let me anywhere near her, but he'll let a killer roam free." Dominic slipped an arm into his jacket sleeve and turned back to the hallway. "I'm not waiting for the killer to pick us off, one by one."

"Tyler is limited in what he can do, Dominic," I said. "He can't investigate an incident he's directly involved in. It's a conflict of interest. He'll need to hand off the investigation to the Shady Creek police. But before that happens, he has to at least contain the crime scene. That means nobody leaves."

Mom gasped. "Cen's right. Tyler—I mean Sheriff Gates—knows what's best. No matter what, you can't go out in the storm. You'll freeze to death!"

Dominic zipped his jacket. "I'd rather take my chances outside than stay here."

Aunt Amber shook her head. "No, you have to stay. No one's in danger because there is no killer. Merlinda's death was an accident. Pearl just messed up with her deadly tea."

"Stop accusing me of murder. Amber." Aunt Pearl snapped. "Why on earth would I harm Merlinda?"

"I-I never said you did it intentionally, Pearl." Aunt Amber looked around uneasily. "Who knows? Maybe it was your tea, or maybe it was Ruby's cake. Something killed Merlinda, and all we know is that it was a terrible accident. Nobody here's a killer, though."

"Get real." Dominic snorted. "The killer is right here in this room. I'm getting help."

"Help from whom?" Mom asked. "You can't make it to Shady Creek with the roads still closed. And we're lucky to have Sheriff Gates right here keeping us safe."

"More like unlucky," Aunt Pearl muttered under her breath.

"Hmphf." Brayden made no secret of his dislike and lack of confidence in Tyler. He would have fired him in an instant if he could. But finding a replacement was pretty much impossible, and firing him would make Brayden a very unpopular mayor. No one else in their right mind wanted to enforce law and order in Westwick Corners.

"We think it's the Christmas cake, Dominic. You ate some too, right?" I put on a worried expression.

"But you just said the cake—" Mom's eyes darted back and forth between Aunt Amber and me.

Aunt Amber nodded. "Cen's right, Dominic. You ate a lot of that cake. You can't go outside alone until we have that cake tested. If you leave and get sick like Merlinda, there won't be anyone there to help you."

While we had pretty much ruled out the cake, Dominic didn't know that. He had been out of the room when Earl confirmed that his rat poison ingredients were safe for humans.

He scoffed. "I'm not worried about it."

"Why not, Dominic?" Aunt Pearl pointed a bony finger at him. "Is it because you killed Merlinda? You did it with that weird green powder you sprinkled on Merlinda's potatoes."

Tyler shook his head. "No. I found the jar. The green stuff is just a health food supplement."

"Never asked you," Aunt Pearl snapped.

"I would never hurt Merlinda," Dominic protested. "I loved her."

"Then why are you in such a hurry to leave your wife?" Aunt Amber asked.

Innocent husbands usually weren't anxious to abandon their deceased wives like discarded luggage. His actions didn't match his words.

Tyler stepped toward Dominic and blocked him. "Nobody goes anywhere until we figure this out. You included."

"But—" Dominic raised his arm to object.

"It's dangerous outside." Tyler tipped his head toward the window. "I know this situation isn't ideal. The fact is that we are all trapped here until the storm lets up. The earliest the Shady Creek medical examiner can get here is tomorrow morning because of the storm. Until she arrives, we all stay."

"Tyler's right, Dominic," Mom waved toward the window. "Look outside. The snow is too deep to walk in, let alone drive."

The wind had sculpted huge snowdrifts that made even driving out of the parking lot impossible. Dominic's abandoned Escalade still sat in the middle of the driveway under a giant mound of snow. Maybe sheer laziness wasn't the only reason he hadn't driven the extra few feet to the parking lot. Maybe he had planned a getaway all along.

Tyler clamped a hand on Dominic's shoulder and steered him to the sofa. "If I were you, I'd sit down and talk so we can solve this thing together. I want to know everything about Merlinda, including her family troubles back home. It's in your own best interest to cooperate because things don't look that good for you right now."

"Am I a suspect?" Dominic didn't sit down. He stood beside the sofa, arms crossed instead. "Or under arrest?"

Tyler rubbed his chin before answering Dominic. "Everybody's a suspect until we have more answers. As her husband, you're suspect number one until you prove otherwise. I will arrest you if you try to leave, Dominic, so don't even bother."

"I knew it," Aunt Pearl muttered under her breath.

Tyler hadn't actually said much of anything to anyone. He was even tight-lipped with me, someone he usually shared investigative details with. A hard lump formed in my throat as I realized that this time I was part of the case and quite possibly a suspect just like the rest of my family. Nobody was ruled out yet. Tyler couldn't compare notes with me even if he wanted to.

Gail smiled sarcastically. "Tough break, Tyler. You really have your hands full. You're waiting for the real police to get here?"

Dominic glared at Gail. "Uh—excuse me. Merlinda just died and you're making jokes? What kind of a person are you?"

"Apparently, not a killer like you," Gail's tone was bitter. "I bet you took out a boatload of insurance on your wife before you killed her."

Brayden covered his ears like a child. "Everybody stop it! You're all giving me a migraine. Just do what Tyler says." Brayden had run for mayor because he liked being in charge. Too bad he was horrible at it. He avoided conflict like the plague. That's what he expected from Tyler as sheriff—to do all of the dirty work. Brayden always took the credit. But when things went haywire, Tyler got all the blame.

I wasn't sure what surprised me more: Brayden's outburst or his siding with Tyler.

Gail scowled at Brayden. "Don't order me around, Brayden."

Brayden let out a deep sigh. "I wasn't ordering anyone—never mind. Just listen to the sheriff."

"Sheriff, you're an idiot." Dominic pointed to Aunt Pearl. "It's that weird tea of hers. What if that old biddy poisons someone else?"

"We'll make sure no one else drinks the tea. Simple enough." Tyler's mouth set into a frown.

Aunt Pearl's whole body shook as she cursed under her breath. Her anger was visible even by candlelight. "You'd all be dead by now if I had wanted to poison you."

Brayden turned to Dominic. "You watch too many crime shows. Pearl's not capable of something like that."

Aunt Pearl shook her fist. "Don't tell me what I'm capable of! I could kill you all without lifting a finger."

"Pearl!" Mom gasped. "Don't talk like that."

It occurred to me that poison was the weapon of choice for little old ladies. I kept that thought to myself.

Aunt Pearl stormed over to Dominic and pounded on his chest. He was at least a foot taller than her so her punches landed somewhere between his stomach and chest. "Why did you have to come here in the first place?"

"You invited me, remember? Stop hitting me." Dominic grabbed Aunt Pearl's bony wrists and held her at arm's-length.

"I only invited you in the first place because I knew you couldn't make it. Merlinda planned to go home. I extended the invitation knowing you wouldn't show up. Except you did."

"She's my wife, Pearl. I don't need an invitation from you to visit her."

"Oh yeah? Well, I happen to know that Melinda already told you she was flying home to Vanuatu. It's a ten-hour flight so why did you expect to even find her here? You couldn't possibly have known ahead of time that her flight was canceled."

"Of course I knew. I checked the extended weather forecast. There was no chance the storm wouldn't hit." Dominic sounded unconvincing. "Science always trumps magic. It even got me a last-minute flight deal."

Aunt Pearl snorted. "Liar. Nobody gets last-minute flight deals at Christmastime."

"The storm forecast came out only hours before Merlinda's departure," Mom added. "How could you have known she'd be stranded here? There's only one daily flight to Vanuatu, and it's on the same plane you supposedly came in on."

Aunt Amber nodded. "Something about your story doesn't add up, Dominic. You must have arrived earlier than today." She muttered something under her breath.

Dominic's anger suddenly vanished. His face went slack and his eyelids drooped. He swayed unsteadily on his feet. He leaned against the wall for support momentarily before slumping down into a sitting position on the floor.

Aunt Amber smiled. "One down."

Brayden jumped up from the sofa and hurried over to steady Dominic. "Dominic? What's wrong?"

No answer.

"What's going on?" Gail followed behind Brayden and leaned over Dominic. "Are you sick too?"

Dominic nodded once before his head drooped down onto his chest.

Aunt Amber repeated her spell, and within seconds Gail and Brayden were bewitched along with Dominic. The three of them slouched together against the wall with Gail in the middle of the two men. They collapsed in on one another in a heap.

"What the heck—" Tyler spun around.

"You're as bad as Aunt Pearl," I stared at our three unconscious guests.

"You can thank me later," Aunt Amber said. "They're too much of a distraction. We need to get to the real issue—Pearl's tea."

"Just stop it, Amber!" Aunt Pearl stomped her foot. "I will not be framed for a crime I didn't commit!"

Tyler shook his head. "Okay, we need to have a frank discussion. You can't just place spells on people willy-nilly, Amber. How will we know what's real and what's supernatural?"

"That's precisely why I froze them," Aunt Amber said. "Remove the variables so we can crack this case."

Tyler shook his head. "I'll worry about solving the case. In the meantime, you need to stop interfering."

"It's as much my business as it is yours, Tyler. We can't expose all our witch secrets or risk the Shady Creek CSI unit going off on a tangent just because they find supernatural things they can't explain. We have to eliminate magic from the equation."

"I'll handle all that," Tyler said. "But in the meantime, hands off. Wake these people up right now."

I shuddered at the thought of Brayden discovering that he had been knocked out by Aunt Amber's spell. There would be hell to pay. He would no doubt find a way to blame Tyler for it too.

"You do realize that Merlinda's supernatural talents could be the reason she was targeted in the first place," Aunt Pearl said. "One of these interlopers is likely Merlinda's killer, not one of us. Either you take action or I will, sheriff. Before someone else ends up dead."

Aunt Pearl no longer seemed any worse for wear from the botched tea. Her bluish skin tone had vanished and she was steady on her feet.

"Relax, Pearl," Mom said. "That goes for you too, Amber. Let the sheriff do his job."

Dominic, Gail, and Brayden all snored peacefully, a cacophony of snorts and whistles.

We had all forgotten about Earl. He stood in the doorway, a puzzled expression on his face. He had changed out of his Santa suit into a flannel shirt and overalls. "Pearl, what the heck's going on? You promised me none of that funny stuff tonight."

Earl meant Aunt Pearl's witchcraft.

"No…I just said I wouldn't do it on you." She noticed our puzzled looks. "Mind your own business!"

"You made it our business, Aunt Pearl." I shook my head in dismay.

Aunt Pearl's business was the very reason we were in this mess in the first place. There was no getting around the fact that Merlinda would probably still be with us if it wasn't for Aunt Pearl's weird Christmas Eve dinner party.

CHAPTER 19

erlinda seemed all but forgotten. Tyler and Aunt Amber argued about the best investigative techniques while our three guests snored on the living room floor.

Tyler acquiesced to Aunt Amber with a little reverse psychology. "You're right, Amber. We have to incapacitate our suspects while we solve the case."

Aunt Amber smiled. "Let's get to it then."

"Wait a minute, sheriff," Aunt Pearl said. "You can't hold Dominic or any of us against our will. What kind of lawman are you? You haven't charged us with anything. You've barely even questioned us."

"The Shady Creek police will do that," Tyler said. "I have to recuse myself because I was here when Merlinda died. I'm part of the case too."

"Probably guilty as sin too," Aunt Pearl muttered under her breath.

Aunt Amber rolled her eyes. "I think we already know who did this to Merlinda, Pearl. Accidents happen and the sooner you own up to—"

"Stop accusing me, Amber! I drank the same tea myself and there's nothing wrong with me." Aunt Pearl turned to Tyler. "As for you,

115

sheriff, even if you wanted to take us into town and lock us all up, you can't. The Westwick Corners jail is too small to hold more than two people. You didn't think of that now, did you, sonny?"

Tyler ignored Aunt Pearl's disrespectful tone and pointed to the snoring lumps propped up against the wall. "They aren't going anywhere for the moment. Amber, how long—?"

"They'll remain asleep as long as you want." Aunt Amber said. "I'll only wake them once you say the word."

"What the heck is going on?" Earl's forehead crinkled into a frown. "Did they drink Pearl's tea too?"

Aunt Pearl stamped her foot. "How many times do I have to tell you people? It's not my tea. I have no idea where that printed recipe came from or how it got into my pocket. Same goes for the copy that Amber found on the kitchen counter. Somebody's trying to frame me. I didn't screw up the ingredients no matter what Amber says."

"The recipe is in your handwriting, Pearl. I would recognize it anywhere." Aunt Amber waved the paper under Aunt Pearl's nose. "Admit it. You made a mistake."

"That's a forgery, Amber. How dare you accuse me of—"

"Oh, just stop bickering, you two!" Mom stepped between her sisters and pushed them apart with her arms. "I'm glad there was nothing wrong with Pearl's tea. That makes it even more important to get to the bottom of things. We have to find out what happened to poor Merlinda, and we won't get anywhere arguing amongst ourselves."

Aunt Pearl and Aunt Amber each took a few steps back and stared at Mom in shock.

I was proud to see Mom standing up to her two strong-willed sisters.

A loud snore shattered the silence.

More of a snort, really.

Dominic opened one eye momentarily before dropping off to sleep again.

Aunt Amber giggled at another loud snore. This time it came from Brayden.

I yawned, feeling sleepy all of a sudden. For the first time, I noticed that we were all lethargic, eyelids drooping and fighting the urge to stay awake. My thoughts wandered at a time that I should have been at rapt attention. Had I been bewitched too?

I rubbed my head and turned to Aunt Pearl. "We really need to figure this out before they wake up."

"Then talk to your sheriff boyfriend over there. Why should we do his job for him?" Aunt Pearl asked.

I glanced at Tyler. He crouched down in the hallway and dropped something into a baggie with a gloved hand.

I turned back to Aunt Pearl. "We're not doing his job for him. We're simply helping him to eliminate useless leads. If we can at least do that, then he can hand over proof we're not involved to the Shady Creek police. Let's find evidence to rule each other out rather than pointing fingers at each other."

"Cen's right." Aunt Amber nodded.

We all stared at the snoring bodies in front of us.

"One of them must be the killer," Mom said.

"Nonsense." Aunt Pearl sighed. "I wish it were true since I despise all of them. But the sad fact is that it's your Christmas cake, Ruby."

"Oh...so now it's my cake?" Mom's hand flew to her chest. "How can that be? You all ate some."

Aunt Pearl shook her head. "No, Ruby. We only pretended to eat it. Just like we have every damn Christmas for the last twenty years."

"What are you saying? That you don't like my cake? That can't be— you guys eat so much I can barely keep up with the baking." Mom turned to me. "Cen, you love my Christmas cake."

"Uh, well...I'm on a low-carb diet so..."

Realization dawned. "You didn't eat any tonight, did you?"

I averted my eyes, ashamed.

Mom turned to Amber. "I suppose you're in on the cake conspiracy too?"

Aunt Amber shrugged, palms out in surrender. "I have to watch my figure, Ruby. As a single gal…"

"I'm sorry, Mom. We know you go to a lot of trouble and…we wanted to spare your feelings." I felt a pang of guilt. The jig was up, Mom's feelings were crushed, all because none of us had the guts to reveal the truth about her inedible cake for years on end. I just couldn't lie anymore.

"Speak for yourself, missy." Aunt Pearl stomped toward the hall. "I'm going to solve this thing once and for all."

"Wait—you can't leave." Tyler blocked her in the doorway. "No one goes anywhere."

"Sheriff or not, you can't hold me here against my will." Aunt Pearl scowled. "Maybe you can corral Dominic, but you can't stop a witch. Come hell or high water, I'm pulling out all the stops to figure out this crime and expose the killer. Somebody has to. It's obviously beyond your capabilities."

Tyler rolled his eyes and his mouth upturned in a slight smile.

Which infuriated Aunt Pearl. "Just try and stop me."

Tyler didn't move.

Aunt Pearl looked confused. Her eyes darted back and forth between Tyler and the front door.

"Sheriff—you gonna stop me or what?" She crossed her arms and planted her feet wide.

I ran into the hallway, followed by Mom and Aunt Amber.

I faced my aunt. "Seriously, Aunt Pearl, where can you go in this storm?"

Aunt Pearl stepped backward until she was against the door. She cowered like a cornered animal, powerless.

"None of your business," Aunt Pearl snapped. Her body belied her sharp words. For the first time, she looked uncertain.

And scared.

CHAPTER 20

It all happened so fast.

Aunt Pearl faced us in a combat stance, her back against the front door.

"Aunt Pearl! Put the gun down!" My arms shot up instinctively. She wouldn't shoot to kill, but I wouldn't put it past her to shoot my foot or possibly an arm or leg if I didn't cooperate. She would rationalize it and repair the damage with witchcraft.

I couldn't afford to take that chance.

"Hey, that's Tyler's gun! What the heck—" Aunt Amber raised her arms as realization dawned. "Pearl, what on earth are you doing?"

My pulse quickened. I scanned the hall for Tyler, but there was no sign of him. He had been right beside Aunt Pearl less than a minute ago. Never mind his gun—what had she done with him?

"We've got a killer in our house and Sheriff Gates carelessly left his gun lying around," Aunt Pearl said. "Someone had to take charge of the situation." She tilted her head toward the floor. Tyler's empty holster lay where he had stood moments earlier.

I kept my voice calm. "And that someone is you?"

Tyler had been wearing his holster with his gun in place, I was sure of that. He was always careful with firearms too. If he wasn't wearing his gun, even for a minute, he locked it up. And if he wasn't wearing it, that meant only one thing.

Aunt Pearl had gotten it by magical means.

And Tyler was in trouble.

My heart caught in my throat. Where exactly *was* Tyler?

Aunt Pearl was becoming unhinged, and I had to stop her before it was too late. Freaking out would only escalate the situation. I needed a strategy to disarm her instead.

My eyes met Aunt Amber's. She was thinking the same thing. She backed away slowly so as to not attract Aunt Pearl's attention, then slipped out into the living room.

"Put the gun down, Pearl." Mom stood behind me.

I couldn't convince Aunt Pearl to disarm but maybe Mom could. Mom rarely confronted her sister, but the current situation demanded action. Mom had my back, literally. I just hoped things didn't escalate further. Sibling rivalry was one thing. Sibling supernatural rivalry was quite another thing altogether.

I frowned. "It's not like Tyler to remove his holster, except when we…" My voice trailed off as I felt eyes upon me.

"Except when you what?" The corners of Aunt Pearl's mouth turned up in a smirk. She held the gun steady. "You want to enlighten us?"

"No." I kept my voice level and calm. "Never mind. Just put that thing down."

Aunt Pearl lowered the gun just as Aunt Amber returned, followed by Tyler. He looked tired and disheveled but otherwise unharmed. Aunt Pearl had obviously incapacitated him with witchcraft in order to steal his gun.

"Hey, that's my gun." Tyler lunged at Aunt Pearl and within seconds disarmed her. He replaced his recovered gun in its holster and put it on. Then he pointed at my two aunts. "You two, go sit in the living room. Amber, make sure she doesn't go anywhere."

Aunt Amber clamped a hand on Aunt Pearl's bony shoulder and steered her toward the doorway.

"Get ready for a lawsuit, Sheriff. This is police harassment." Aunt Pearl paused in the doorway and swore under her breath.

Tyler ignored her.

"C'mon, Pearl." Aunt Amber pulled Aunt Pearl into the living room.

Aunt Pearl lunged toward the doorway. "You can't order me around, Sheriff. I'll go wherever I like."

"No you won't." Aunt Amber guided Aunt Pearl to the sofa with an iron grip. They both sat down.

I was relieved that Tyler was okay but fearful that Aunt Pearl had taken the extreme measure of tricking Tyler when we already faced a killer in our midst. Witchcraft and weaponry were a deadly combination. Aunt Pearl knew very well that she had taken things too far. What the heck was wrong with her?

"She's not going anywhere," Aunt Amber yelled to Tyler in the hall. She turned to Aunt Pearl. "The sheriff hasn't arrested you, but that doesn't mean I can't. You're under WICCA house arrest, Pearl."

"You're arresting your own sister?" Grandma Vi hovered above the dining room sideboard. She looked at her daughters in disdain. "Amber, really…that's an abuse of power. Can't you two girls get along for once?"

I smiled despite the gravity of the situation. My geriatric aunts were forever young girls in Grandma Vi's eyes.

Our bickering woke Brayden but not Dominic and Gail who still snoozed peacefully.

Brayden rubbed his temple and frowned. He had overheard snippets of the conversation. "Tyler gave you his gun?"

Aunt Pearl nodded. "He didn't give me his gun. I stole it."

"Tyler! Get over here," Brayden barked.

Tyler appeared in the doorway. "Yes?"

Brayden turned to face him. "Is what Pearl says true? You got tricked by a little old lady?"

Aunt Pearl glared at Brayden. "I'm not old."

Tyler began to speak, only to be interrupted by Aunt Amber.

"Leave Tyler out of this," Aunt Amber said. "You know what Pearl is capable of, Brayden. Aside from that, stealing a gun isn't the worst thing that's happened here. Not by a long shot."

"You mean Merlinda? The sheriff should have prevented that too. Merlinda was killed right under his watch." Brayden shook his head in disgust.

"You were there too. We all were." I neglected to mention that Brayden had been unconscious at the time. Because it was a spell, he remained blissfully unaware of that fact.

"Maybe so, but I didn't do a single thing to contribute to tonight's tragedy." Brayden worried about himself first and political fallout second. Anything and anyone else placed a distant third. As far as he was concerned, Merlinda's tragic death wasn't really his concern. Death had quickly cured him of his infatuation.

"I strongly disagree. None of this would have happened without you, Brayden," Aunt Pearl said. "You provoked Dominic, and then he killed Merlinda in a fit of jealousy."

"That's a lie. I barely even noticed Merlinda." Brayden's eye twitched, a sure sign he was lying.

I glanced over to where Gail and Dominic were still passed out against the wall, nestled awkwardly into each other.

There was no sign of Earl, though. He must have made himself scarce when Aunt Pearl grabbed Tyler's gun.

"Quit changing the subject, Pearl," Tyler said. "And keep your hands off my gun. We've all had enough drama for one night."

"Well, next time, don't leave your gun lying around, sheriff." Aunt Pearl snapped. "I can't be held accountable for your carelessness."

"But I didn't—oh, never mind." Tyler turned away. "I've got more important things to do than argue with you, Pearl. I know I never removed my holster or my gun."

Mom frowned. "Keep messing with Tyler and you'll have to answer to me, Pearl. Got it?"

"Got it." Aunt Pearl sighed, defeated. She was outmatched by her two sisters for once.

Grandma Vi floated a foot above Tyler's head. She winked at me and whispered, "Ooh…magic."

I ignored her. "Let's talk about Merlinda. We were all here at the table and ate most of the same things. Nobody left the table, except for Merlinda. How could she have been poisoned? By something slow-acting? If so, then she could have ingested it hours earlier."

Mom and I exchanged nervous glances. I knew that despite Earl's explanation, she was still a little worried about the flour she had used for the Christmas cake. Mom had absolutely nothing to gain from Merlinda's demise though. And everything to lose, with a guest dying at our Inn. She would be quickly eliminated as a suspect.

On the other hand, Mom was a known expert in herbal potions, some of which were actually poisonous. She was also the Inn's cook and had prepared all of Merlinda's meals. She had the means and opportunity to poison Merlinda but no real motive. Still, the police would have to investigate her in the absence of any other leads. We needed to explore all those leads in order to rule her out.

I flashed back to the green powder that Dominic had given Merlinda. He could have added something to the health food supplement. Maybe it was tainted with a hidden ingredient just like Mom's cake was.

But maybe Dominic's powder wasn't tainted with something harmless like peanut butter. As Merlinda's husband, he certainly had a motive.

I turned to Tyler. "What about Merlinda's room? Maybe there is something there that could have harmed her?"

"Let's go." He headed upstairs with Mom and me close behind.

CHAPTER 21

Ten minutes later Tyler, Mom, and I stood in the doorway of Merlinda's room. We had inspected her room, being careful not to touch anything. Her suite was spotless and devoid of personal items. The only sign of Merlinda was her purse, which sat atop a neatly made single bed. Other than a few toiletries and clothes in the bureau drawers, there was little evidence that the room was occupied, let alone signs of Merlinda's three-month stay.

Tyler and I had to at least probe the supernatural leads so the Shady Creek police didn't start the investigation by chasing red herrings. It wasn't exactly by the book, but it was necessary with four witches and a ghost in the mix.

"It's kind of strange that Merlinda had no pictures or mementos of Dominic." Tyler rummaged through Merlinda's purse. He pulled out her phone and studied the screen. He held it up for us to see. "Her screen picture is of another man. Not Dominic, her new husband. Most people keep some reminder of their significant other when they're away from home."

"Maybe she kept the pictures hidden away on her computer because she didn't want questions." I could understand Merlinda hiding pictures of their secret wedding, but there wasn't a single photograph of Dominic anywhere in the room. Then again, she had kept him secret from us too.

Tyler dumped the contents of Merlinda's purse on the bed. He sifted through her wallet with a gloved hand. He turned up nothing but a lipstick tube, a small amount of cash, and a Vanuatu passport. "Not even a wallet picture of the wedding. If that part is actually true."

"Maybe they weren't as serious as Dominic claimed. Merlinda could have just played along with the wedding story." I recalled Merlinda's odd behavior. "Could the marriage be a sham?"

Merlinda hadn't exactly seemed enamored of Dominic. In fact, she had seemed shocked by his arrival. If it was a marriage of convenience, only Dominic could tell us what that convenience was. Except he wasn't talking.

We searched the rest of the room—or rather Tyler did while I videotaped his search with my cellphone. He had turned up nothing but an empty teacup with a smattering of still-damp tea leaves. It must have been Aunt Pearl's tea from earlier in the day. Tyler placed the cup in a plastic baggie with his gloved hand.

I just couldn't fathom who had wanted Merlinda dead. Certainly not Aunt Pearl. Her star student was a walking advertisement for Pearl's Charm School. In fact, the short time Merlinda had spent in Westwick Corners had revolved around Pearl's Charm School, and she had kept to herself most of the time. She had no local friends and until tonight, barely even spoke to anyone. She hadn't even met Brayden before tonight. I kept going back to Dominic. He had to be involved somehow.

"What's the slowest acting poison around?" I asked.

Tyler shrugged. "I don't know. What I do know is that anything lethal normally triggers a quick reaction, like within minutes. Something slow-acting would have produced symptoms over a longer period of time. It wouldn't result in the sudden reaction Merlinda had."

"That's right," Mom said. "Herbal tinctures work exactly the same way."

"Merlinda was just fine until dinnertime," I said. "No symptoms or complaints."

Something else troubled me. Merlinda had been a last-minute addition to our Christmas Eve celebration since she had planned to be a on a flight home. She was only here because her holiday plans had fallen through. If it was a crime of opportunity, who stood to gain?

None of us, except possibly Dominic. As her newly wedded husband, he probably stood to inherit. Merlinda's family was fabulously wealthy.

Come to think of it, Westwick Corners was the perfect place to do away with Merlinda. Few knew her here, and those that did would just assume she had gone home for the holidays. Only the people in this house knew that she had missed her flight.

We headed out into the hallway. As I shut Merlinda's door behind me, it slammed shut with much more force than I had used. In the same instant, a gust of wind blew toward us. I ran to the stairs with Tyler and Mom close behind me.

Tyler and I exchanged glances as we stared down the stairs to the front door. The door was wide open and banged against the wall with each new gust. The wind swirled around and fluttered the papers on the hall table out onto the empty porch.

Another storm was brewing, and I felt powerless to stop it.

CHAPTER 22

I stood on the front porch with Mom and Tyler. The snow had stopped falling, but it was still bitterly cold with a biting wind.

"Hey, look at this." I pointed to the footprints that started on the porch and led down the stairs. They were women's footprints. Since Mom stood beside me, they had to belong to either Gail or one of my aunts.

Dominic's Cadillac Escalade was missing too.

Aunt Pearl.

I ran into the living room and found Aunt Amber struggling to free herself. She was tied to a chair with a string of Christmas tree lights.

Earl walked in from the dining room at the same time. "What the heck—?"

My heart thumped in my chest as I scanned the room. Gail was now awake and sat in the armchair. But Dominic was gone.

Gail, unlike Aunt Amber, was unrestrained. She played a game on her phone, so engrossed that she didn't even look up. Or maybe she was purposely ignoring us.

"What happened?" I quickly untied Aunt Amber's hands and feet while Tyler, Earl, and Mom searched the house for any sign of Aunt Pearl and Dominic.

"Pearl tied me up, and now she's on the run." Aunt Amber glared at Gail as she rose to her feet. "Thanks for nothing, Gail."

Gail shrugged. "Why would I help you? You knocked me out cold." She turned back to her phone screen.

"Where did Dominic go?" I asked.

Aunt Amber shrugged. "I don't know. He must be with Pearl. She knocked me unconscious before she tied me up, so I didn't see what happened. Next thing I knew he was gone too."

My mouth dropped open. "She kidnapped him?"

"Either that or he kidnapped her. Or maybe they're in cahoots with each other." Aunt Amber sighed. "I just don't know anymore. Pearl's acting so weird."

It also struck me as odd that Aunt Pearl had used a string of Christmas lights instead of witchcraft to restrain Aunt Amber. On the one hand, it was probably more effective to tie up Aunt Amber than rely upon a spell she could potentially undo. On the other hand, Aunt Pearl always claimed she could out-spell anyone, including Aunt Amber. Her use of physical restraints seemed a little out of character.

Aunt Amber followed behind me as I headed back to the front porch.

"Pearl knows it's her tea," she said. "You saw her get sick from it too. She's guilty as sin."

"It was an honest mistake." I couldn't believe that Aunt Pearl planned to kill Merlinda on purpose, by accident, or otherwise. I flashed back to her milk thistle, or rather, mistletoe, tea remedy. She had hidden most of her symptoms, but the tea had sickened her too. "If it was a mistake, then why didn't she just own up to it?"

"She'll never admit that, Cen." Aunt Amber sighed. "She'd rather be a fugitive from justice."

Mom confirmed our worst fears when she returned to the front porch, breathless. "She's gone. We've looked upstairs, downstairs, everywhere. We've got to find her."

Aunt Pearl was AWOL. She had stymied the investigation, held us at gunpoint, and now she was a fugitive on the run.

It was a dumb move. Her negligence wouldn't attract new students once the secret got out. Which it was sure to now that she was a missing person.

Instead, her incriminating behavior implied she had intentionally poisoned her own student.

Brayden joined us. "I checked the basement but there's no sign of Pearl. She could be anywhere. Running away makes her look guilty."

Brayden was right about that, but I was more worried about Aunt Pearl's survival. She was still weak from the poisoned tea, and with hardly any body fat, she wouldn't survive in the frigid temperature outside.

What really troubled me was how Aunt Pearl had tied up Aunt Amber. Was that a sign that her supernatural abilities had decreased from the effects of her tea? If she had resorted to using mortal restraints to tie up Aunt Amber, then her witchcraft was either compromised or possibly no longer worked at all. Or even worse, maybe the poison made her spells go haywire with serious, even deadly, unintended results.

I turned to Mom. "I don't think Aunt Pearl is firing on all cylinders, if you know what I mean."

Mom was frantic. "I'm afraid I do. Pearl isn't being rational. Who drinks their own poison just to prove a point?"

Aunt Amber sighed. "That's Pearl, I guess. She always has to be right no matter what the consequences. Even if those consequences result in her undoing." She shivered and pulled her shawl tighter around her shoulders.

Tyler and Earl stepped onto the porch. Tyler talked into his cell phone, providing details of Aunt Pearl's escape to the Shady Creek Police. He put his phone back in his pocket. "I've alerted the Shady

Creek police, though I doubt it will do much good. The roads are still closed, so she can't drive anywhere."

Earl slowly shook his head. "I doubt she took the Escalade. You know how Pearl hates driving."

I had to agree with Earl. Aside from the impassable roads, driving wasn't Aunt Pearl's favored mode of transport. That's exactly what worried me. Teleporting while impaired from the tea could have unintended results. The thought of her airborne and hell-bent on revenge was troubling to say the least. Aunt Pearl could be anywhere.

Tyler's eyes met mine, his face tinged with worry. His sheriff abilities, no matter how good, couldn't hold a candle to a desperate witch on the run.

"We'll find her somehow," I reassured him. As a witch, Aunt Pearl had plenty of travel options. That meant she was unlikely to freeze to death, but she could certainly get into a whack of trouble.

"Being on the run really complicates things," Mom said. "I never figured Pearl would be a fugitive from justice."

"Me neither," Aunt Amber agreed. "What can we do?"

Tyler patted Mom's shoulder in reassurance, but his expression remained doubtful. "I doubt Pearl planned ahead, so she probably won't go far. We'll find her. The Shady Creek police have an all-points bulletin out."

"She could have an accomplice waiting somewhere." Brayden's attempt at helpfulness fell flat. He was trying to help in his own weird way, but his suggestion only upset us even more. He was already convinced of her guilt.

Earl's face fell as realization dawned. Pearl had left him behind too. "I was supposed to be her partner in crime, but nothing turned out as planned."

"Huh?" Tyler frowned. "What do you mean by partner in crime?"

"You think I wanted to wear that dumb Santa suit?" He shook his head. "Uh-uh. Pearl made me do it. She told me that everybody else was getting dressed up for the costume party. Except I was the only one. She tricked me."

Mom nodded. "She's good at talking people into things they would never do otherwise. Though I have to say, Earl, you really did look the part."

Earl sighed. "Was it something I said? One minute she was here. Then the next…gone."

Mom patted his arm. "It's not you, Earl. She does stuff like this all the time. You'll get used to it."

Though Earl had farmed on the outskirts of Westwick Corners all his life, only recently had he kindled a friendship with Aunt Pearl. That friendship had quickly turned romantic. They made a strange couple. Aunt Pearl was ornery and dramatic, while Earl was calm, romantic, and easygoing. Maybe it was a case of opposites attract.

"She's gone, all right." Brayden pointed at the petite footprints in the snow that ended across the driveway.

The tracks didn't stop where Dominic's Escalade had been parked. They continued onto the other side of the driveway. Maybe the footprints, and the missing SUV, were all for show, a diversion tactic. While the poisoned tea had probably wreaked havoc with her powers, we couldn't be sure of that.

As long as Aunt Pearl was functioning normally, she could go anywhere. She could transport herself through portals with a little effort and a bit of magic. I doubted she was far away, though. In fact, it wouldn't surprise me if she were watching us right now.

I scanned the garden and the parking lot for any sign of her but saw nothing.

Gail, her phone game finished, joined us on the porch. She put her arm around Brayden's waist and steered him a few feet away so they were a safe distance from Aunt Amber.

"Pearl knows that everyone makes mistakes," Mom said. "She's just incriminating herself by running away. I wish I could just talk some sense into her." She spoke louder than usual. Like me, she probably suspected that Aunt Pearl was hiding nearby.

Brayden snorted at the thought. He jabbed his thumb in Tyler's direction. "Too late for that. How could he let her get away like that?"

"You could have stopped her too," I pointed out. "You saw her leave."

Brayden shrugged. "Not my job. I'm not the sheriff."

"Oh, for crying out loud, Brayden. Take ownership for once." Aunt Amber said. "We're all in this together."

"No, we're not, and don't criticize me, Amber. I wish Gail and I had never come here in the first place. You and your crazy family…" Brayden threw up his hands before pressing his palm firmly onto Gail's back. He steered her toward the door. "C'mon Gail. Let's go inside."

Brayden's indifference was the final straw. His self-centeredness remained in full force, even after Merlinda's death. He didn't seem to care that Pearl was missing and possibly freezing to death. He lacked compassion for anyone but himself. He berated Tyler, criticized Aunt Pearl, and barely lifted a finger to help anyone. And to think I had almost married him. While I was glad to have dodged a bullet on that one, I was furious at Brayden's thoughtlessness.

Brayden paused at the door. He let go of Gail and motioned for her to enter ahead of him.

I fought to contain my anger, but I was so enraged that before I knew it, I was whispering the transport spell under my breath. I just wanted Brayden and his self-absorption gone.

As in far-away gone, like Vanuatu. That would serve him right. I pictured him running frantically up and down the beach in a state of confusion, yelling for help.

I knew the spell by heart—I had practiced it for hundreds of hours without success. Reciting it was harmless enough since I wasn't actually capable of enacting the spell. I often said it as a form of witch-swearing. I channeled my anger into an almost mindless incantation:

Make yourself scarce and go away
Don't dilly dally, be on your way
Up, up, and away you go
Far from here to a place I know

Aunt Amber gasped. "Cendrine, what on earth are you doing?"

"Hey, what the—" Gail's voice wavered before she went silent. Her lips moved but no sound came out.

My timing was a little off, because Brayden had still been touching Gail's arm at the exact moment my spell was cast. The couple faded into transparent silhouettes before us.

Then…*Poof!*

They were gone.

Just like that.

"Oh no! It's never worked for me before…" I stood trance-like and stared at the empty doorway where Brayden and Gail had stood seconds earlier.

I had practiced the spell hundreds of times without success. Now, when I hadn't even tried very hard, it had worked flawlessly. Not only had it worked, it had taken two people at once. I was stunned.

Earl jumped backwards, surprisingly fast for a seventy-year-old. "Did you see that? Brayden and Gail just vaporized! Where the heck did they go?"

"Cendrine, bring them back!" Mom pleaded, but it was too late.

"I-I can't! I don't even know what I did. It's never worked before, so I must have done something different this time. I just don't know what it is."

I was still so completely focused on the spell, so stunned that it had actually worked, that I repeated it as I tried to figure out what went wrong.

Poof! Poof!

The same sound as moments earlier, but no sign of the couple.

If I couldn't figure out what I had done, how on earth could I ever bring them back?

$\mathcal{E}$arl rubbed his eyes and shook his head. "What the heck was in your eggnog, Amber? I don't feel so good all of a sudden. You saw it too, right?" He searched our faces for an answer.

We all remained silent. Too bad we couldn't give him one.

Earl sighed. "Great. Now my eyes are playing tricks on me."

It troubled me that we had three suspected poisons, and each pointed to a member of my family. In fact, I was the only witch not connected to a suspicious food or beverage.

Aunt Pearl's poisoned tea, Aunt Amber's spiked eggnog, and Mom's poison-laced Christmas cake created more questions than answers. And the answers started with Aunt Pearl, who was now missing. I feared where those answers could lead us, but we had to know the truth.

We had moved inside to the living room so we wouldn't freeze to death while we figured out how to locate Brayden and Gail.

Earl rubbed his forehead. "You didn't see what I saw? I had the weirdest hallucination. Brayden and Gail faded away into nothingness, just like that." He snapped his fingers for effect. Funny how ordinary people interpreted witchcraft when there was no other logical explanation.

"How odd." Mom's voice was flat, but the corners of her mouth turned up in an involuntary smile.

Mom was secretly proud of me, though she tried not to show it. I was pleased too. I had successfully executed an advanced spell on my own without any help. Now was no time to gloat, though. My focus was on getting Brayden and Gail back.

"Where did they go?" Earl scanned the living room. "I didn't just imagine it, did I?"

"Um, no." I was at a loss for words and so, apparently, was everybody else.

"Merlinda dies, Pearl disappears, and now Brayden and Gail are missing." Earl's voice cracked. "Geez, am I next?"

Mom shook her head. "Of course not, Earl. You'll be fine. But stay inside the house just in case, okay?"

I slipped my arm into Earl's and guided him to the sofa. "Mom's right, Earl. Why don't you relax a little?"

Earl frowned and sat down. "I'm worried about Pearl, Cen. You know how she gets these crazy ideas. What if she's gone off and done something dangerous?" His affection for ornery Aunt Pearl was so sweet. It practically bordered on sainthood.

"I'm sure she'll turn up, Earl. Don't you worry," Mom said in a soothing voice. "She'll be back before you know it."

Earl wiped his brow with the back of his hand. "No more booze this year. It does something terrible to my head."

It was just as well that Earl thought he was seeing things instead of witnessing magic. He'd question that assumption if I didn't bring Brayden and Gail back quickly, though. You'd think that between Mom, Aunt Amber, and me we could figure out how to reverse my spell. But apparently, three witches aren't any more powerful than one.

What we really needed was the antidote, or reversal spell. Trouble was, this spell couldn't be undone by another witch. That self-protecting mechanism was designed so that one witch couldn't interfere with another witch's spell, either on purpose or otherwise.

That witch was me.

The only problem was that I had no clue how to fix things. While I had practiced the spell many times, I hadn't mastered it. Not by a long shot. Minor variations in the original spell meant modifications to the reversal spell too. Aunt Pearl hadn't even shown me the reversal spell yet.

Aunt Pearl.

We had to find her, and fast. What if she had somehow been caught up in my spell? If she had been standing nearby and I hadn't noticed… No, that couldn't be it. Others had stood much closer to Brayden and Gail, and they were still here. I had no idea where to even start looking for any of them.

Aunt Amber paced back and forth in the living room. "Tell me exactly what you did, Cen. Every single detail. Maybe, just maybe, I can help you reverse everything. I doubt I can, but it's worth a shot."

Her lack of confidence worried me. Another witch couldn't undo this particular spell, so she would have to teach it to me. As the spellcaster, only I could bring them back. To do that I had to master the reversal spell, but how could I possibly do that in time? I had to learn in a matter of minutes what normally took months of practice.

"I have no idea what happened," I said. "All I did was recite the words Aunt Pearl taught me. I wasn't even trying hard, so I never expected it to work." The reason the spell had actually worked this time could be due to anything. A blink of an eye, a slight movement of my hand, or maybe even how I pronounced the words. All I remembered was that I had stood with my weight more on my right foot than my left. But that couldn't be it. I was at a loss as to what I had done differently compared to my prior failed attempts.

I walked over to the Christmas tree and stared at Merlinda's tropical snow globe. I squinted and peered inside hoping against hope. Brayden and Gail were nowhere to be seen. Aunt Pearl wasn't there, either. The tropical paradise appeared the same as before: a white sandy beach dotted with palm trees bordering the ocean. It was troubling since that beach was where I thought I had sent Brayden and, accidentally, Gail. But they weren't there. Where had they gone instead?

"You did your best, and that's what counts, dear." Mom was encouraging even at the worst of times. "Just visualize them when they disappeared and concentrate on their faces. You can do it."

"You really did make them disappear." Earl sat at the far corner of the sofa, arms crossed. For the first time I noticed that his hair was dishevelled, and he looked as though he had just survived the perimeter of a bomb blast. He was completely freaked out. "All this craziness must run in the family. Pearl's done some crazy crap, but this takes the cake."

"Don't worry about it, Earl," Aunt Amber said. "Cen knows what she's doing."

Aunt Amber leaned in close and said to me, "You better know what you're doing."

Actually, I didn't, and I felt terrible for scaring Earl. I had no words to reassure him, but just being around Aunt Pearl should have prepared him for anything. I refocused on the emergency at hand. "I really screwed up, didn't I? How will we find them?"

"We just need to figure out what went wrong with your spell, Cen," Mom said. "Where did you intend to send them?"

"To Merlinda's globe. It was only supposed to be temporary." As I stared at the globe, I felt this weird force repelling me. It felt opposite to the pull of a magnet. In fact, it was more like the repulsive force field of two magnets being pushed together. The globe had an opposing force. Whenever I neared the globe, the strange force pushed me away.

It suddenly dawned on me that there wasn't anything wrong with my spell. It had worked just fine, only to be counteracted by a much stronger force. Merlinda's. I suspected I wasn't the first to fail.

Aunt Pearl hadn't intended to send me outside in a blizzard to freeze to death. She had planned something entirely different, only her spell had hit a stronger opposing force just as mine had.

Aunt Pearl meant to send me into Merlinda's Vanuatu snow globe when something or someone interfered. Of course. Like any expert witch, Merlinda had placed a protective shield around her tropical snow globe to prevent unauthorized entry.

Merlinda's protective shield hadn't only prevented anyone from gaining access to her Vanuatu snow globe. The protective shield was so strong that it had also repelled those who came close and sent them in the opposite direction. I hadn't been close enough to the globe to notice the force before.

What Merlinda had lacked in years of sorcery experience was more than compensated by the sheer strength of her magic. In fact, her witchcraft was strong enough to not only counteract Aunt Pearl's spell but also to send me in a totally different direction.

I had ended up in the wrong place when I had landed outside in the freezing cold. The same thing must have happened to Brayden and Gail too. Aunt Pearl hadn't owned up to her misdirection because she had been too embarrassed to admit that her spell had gone awry.

Only her spell hadn't misfired at all. It had been counteracted by Merlinda's magic.

I ran to the living room window and scanned the yard and driveway for any sign of the pair. They had to be outside somewhere nearby.

I focused my gaze in the same general direction of where Aunt Pearl's spell had sent me earlier.

A flash of movement caught my eye but disappeared just as quickly before I could get a better look. Then nothing. My pulse quickened. "Somebody's hiding by the lawn ornaments."

"That better be Pearl. I'll go check." Earl jumped from the sofa and ran outside.

He returned within minutes, gripping a shivering Aunt Pearl by the arm. "Look who I found. Turns out she was close by after all."

"I told you not to tell anyone." Aunt Pearl shook her arm loose from Earl's grip but seemed secretly pleased that he had rescued her. A pool of water formed at her feet from her dripping wet green velvet pantsuit. "Just like before, you had to go and mess things up."

Mom gasped. "Pearl! Don't talk to Earl like that. He just saved you from freezing to death."

Earl waved his arm in dismissal. "Blame me all you want, Pearl. You're the one who asked me to set up the Santa sleigh in the first place. Not my fault."

"Wait—what happened before?" I turned to Aunt Pearl. "You mean when you were out-spelled by Merlinda?"

"Absolutely not!" Aunt Pearl sat on the edge of the sofa and leaned over to roll up her pant legs. "Nothing went wrong with my spell. Earl wasn't supposed to be by the sleigh. That's why everything got screwed up."

Realization dawned on me as I turned to Earl. "You were Santa in the sleigh outside!"

Earl shrugged. "I was just doing what Pearl told me to. I wanted to add a few finishing touches."

"Yesterday, Earl. You were supposed to have those lawn ornaments finished yesterday." Aunt Pearl always had to get the last word.

Innocent bystanders who were too close to the action had altered both of our spells. In my case, Aunt Pearl's transport spell was intended to send me to Merlinda's tropical snow globe. Instead, I had landed outside on the lawn where Earl was still working on the Santa sleigh. I guessed that Aunt Pearl had been thinking about Earl when she had cast her spell.

But what about my case? I couldn't remember thinking about anything other than wanting to banish Brayden to Vanuatu, and Gail had simply been collateral damage because she had been standing too close to him.

Merlinda's globe had a redirection safeguard built in. It was designed to ensure that no one else could enter her tropical snow globe. But it didn't just repel intruders. Her spell packed such a punch that it sent would-be intruders off in a completely different direction.

But if that was the case, where had Gail and Brayden gone? They weren't outside like Aunt Pearl and I had been.

Someone was lying, and I had no doubt who it was. But now wasn't the time for petty arguments. We had to find Brayden and Gail before it was too late.

CHAPTER 24

"You gonna lock me up, sheriff?" Aunt Pearl stood defiantly in front of Tyler, arms crossed.

"Nope," Tyler chuckled. "Nothing to worry about. You're a terrible escape artist."

"Help me find Brayden and Gail, Aunt Pearl," I pleaded. "Tell me what to do."

"I don't know, Cen. What's in it for me?" Aunt Pearl tapped her foot as she waited for an answer.

I didn't bite.

I was tired of going in circles with Aunt Pearl and never getting anywhere. With or without her help, I would get Brayden and Gail back. I ran to the hall table and motioned for Mom and Aunt Amber to follow. There was no time to waste.

"Ready, Cen?" Aunt Amber handed me a scrap of paper. "I wrote it out for you. All you have to do is visualize them while you recite the words."

I squeezed my eyes shut and recited the reversal spell, imagining Brayden and Gail at the doorway as they had been earlier. The required concentration coupled with the almost instant hangover effects of too much Christmas cheer had given me a splitting headache. If I could somehow get it to work, I promised myself I would never cast another spell. They were incredibly hard to undo and nothing but trouble. I simply wasn't cut out to be a witch.

Aunt Pearl swore under her breath. "You can call off the dogs, sheriff. Just be glad I decided to cooperate so you won't get fired."

Tyler shrugged. He spoke softly into his cell phone before slipping it back into his shirt pocket. His eyes scanned the front lawn as he pointed excitedly to a spot near the Santa sleigh lawn decorations. "Hey, what's that? Something just moved."

"It's Brayden and Gail!" Mom clasped her hands together. "Cen, you did it! You got them back."

I followed Tyler's gaze to the Santa sleigh lawn decoration. Sure enough, Brayden and Gail were there. They were surrounded by a giant glass globe that also enclosed the sleigh. I couldn't believe how large the globe was. But there was no time to gloat.

Gail cowered near Santa's sleigh while Brayden pounded on the glass several feet away.

"Well, they're back on the lawn at least. I still have to get them out of the globe." I sighed.

They waved their arms and clawed at an invisible glass barrier as they mouthed words we couldn't hear. Just like me earlier, they were trapped inside the magical glass globe that surrounded the lawn decorations. So close, but yet, so far away.

On the bright side, at least the snow globe's return meant that we could see them. And that meant a much better chance of actually breaking them free from their glass prison.

It dawned on me that Aunt Pearl had never been trapped in my glass globe in the first place. If she had, Earl couldn't have rescued her. The glass globe that imprisoned Brayden and Gail remained intact, and one spell meant one glass globe.

Why had Aunt Pearl pretended to be caught up in my spell? I had no idea why. What I did know was that my spell hadn't saved Aunt

Pearl after all. Also, my powers were only strong enough to bring the globe back into view. They weren't enough to extract Brayden and Gail from it.

I felt hopeless. If I hadn't actually saved Aunt Pearl, how on earth could I rescue Brayden and Gail?

e stood in the living room by the Christmas tree. Merlinda's snow globe seemed to taunt us from its perch on the Christmas tree. It still emitted an ethereal glow, but the magical quality was gone. Now it just seemed eerie and sad.

Mom's eyes met mine in sympathy. Aunt Pearl and Aunt Amber ignored the globe, seemingly oblivious to its fading glory.

I resisted the temptation to inch closer to the globe. I had no desire to see what was happening in Vanuatu. With Merlinda gone, it hardly mattered anymore.

I asked as nicely as I could. "Aunt Pearl, please help me reverse the rest of the spell."

"You'll never learn unless you apply yourself, Cen," she said. "Don't expect me to do everything for you."

I was sick and tired of Aunt Pearl's tough love. "But what about Brayden and Gail? We can't leave them trapped outside in the globe. They'll freeze to death."

Aunt Amber shook her head. "No, they'll be fine inside the globe. They can wait a few more minutes. Pearl has something to say, don't you, Pearl?" She looked expectantly at her sister.

"Nope." Aunt Pearl crossed her arms and stared at the ceiling as she tapped her foot. "I don't know what you're talking about."

"Yes, you do, and you're going to tell Tyler…I mean, Sheriff Gates, everything you've been up to with Merlinda." A hiccup interrupted Aunt Amber's stern expression. It was a side effect of her alcohol-laced eggnog. She had resumed drinking once Brayden and Gail reappeared.

Aunt Pearl made a zipping motion across her mouth. "My lips are sealed. I'm gonna lawyer up before I incriminate myself."

"Ah ha! You admit there was something wrong with your tea after all." Like a dog with a bone, Aunt Amber never let up.

"Don't be ridiculous." Aunt Pearl paused for a moment. "Okay, maybe I spiked it a little, but not with anything deadly."

I gasped. "You poisoned Merlinda on purpose!"

"Geesh, Cen. You make it sound so sinister. All I did—if I did anything at all—was to help Merlinda out of a jam."

"Then tell us what you did," Tyler demanded. "If you haven't done anything wrong, then you have nothing to worry about."

Aunt Pearl shook her head. "No way. I don't trust you one bit, sheriff. Besides, anything that happened between Merlinda and me is none of your business."

"But Merlinda's dead," I said. "You owe us an explanation, Aunt Pearl. I also need your help to get Brayden and Gail out of the globe before we lose them too. Before it's too late."

"First things first," Aunt Amber turned to Tyler. "If Pearl won't tell you, I will. She told me everything."

Aunt Pearl glared at her sister, aghast. "I'm sure as heck not going to stay here and listen to your made-up stories, Amber. Especially not when you're stinking drunk."

"Don't even think about going anywhere, Pearl," Tyler said. "We need to talk."

"I'll do whatever I like. You can't keep me here." Aunt Pearl turned to leave.

"Maybe not but I can." Mom snapped her fingers and murmured

something in a low voice.

Aunt Pearl yawned and shuffled over to the sofa and sat down. Within seconds she was fast asleep, snoring.

Grandma Vi hovered nearby. "Nicely done, Ruby. I've never seen her so peaceful."

I shook my head. "Wait—what about Brayden and Gail? I still need Aunt Pearl's help to free them from the snow globe."

Tyler frowned. He couldn't see or hear my ghostly grandma.

"Oh, just relax, Cen," Grandma Vi said. "You don't need Pearl. I may be a ghost, but I'm still the best witch around. Who do you think taught Pearl everything in the first place?"

"So you'll help me?" I no longer cared whether Tyler or Earl heard me or not. Let them think I was crazily talking to myself. It was worth it to get Brayden and Gail back before it was too late.

I had never seen Grandma Vi do much magic at all, while living or dead. She had retired before I was born. She always got her daughters to do everything for her, mostly Pearl. Grandma Vi often made promises she couldn't keep. I just hoped this wasn't one of them.

"I'll consider it," Grandma Vi said. "What's in it for me?"

This time I decided not to answer and alarm Tyler further. Instead, I turned to Aunt Amber. "Okay, spill the beans, and tell us what Aunt Pearl was doing with Merlinda."

Aunt Amber talked for fifteen minutes straight. When she finished, we were all too stunned to speak. She was the last person I had expected a teary-eyed confession from.

I felt betrayed. Aunt Pearl had made grandiose plans for a global Pearl's Charm School franchise with Merlinda as her partner. It wasn't something I ever wanted, but I was hurt that she hadn't even asked me.

"You knew all about Pearl and Merlinda's business plans, and you didn't say a word all this time?" Tyler frowned as he jotted something down on his notepad. He leaned forward and waited for Aunt Amber to elaborate.

"Is this where you read me my rights?" Aunt Amber glanced back and forth between Tyler and me, fearful of what lay in store for her. "Am I under arrest?"

Tyler sighed. "Not unless you committed a crime. Did you?"

"Of course not! How can you say such a thing?" Aunt Amber crossed her arms and tried to contain her anger. "I pleaded with Pearl to tell you. When she didn't, it left me in a bit of a pickle. Do I betray my own sister? Or snitch only to be accused of murder myself?"

"Nobody accused you of murder. You could be an accessory to a crime, though." I sensed Aunt Amber still wasn't being completely honest. I glanced over at Aunt Pearl who snored peacefully on the sofa.

"You mean, like aiding and abetting Pearl?" Aunt Amber shook her head. "I had nothing to do with her plan, at least not directly. I don't see why I should incriminate myself just because Pearl won't cooperate."

My face flushed. "Nothing's going to happen to you if you tell the truth, Aunt Amber. We do need to figure out what's going on though. Just tell Tyler what you know, and you won't be in trouble."

"Cen's right," Tyler said. "We need to get to the bottom of this."

"After that, maybe you'll help me free Brayden and Gail," I said hopefully.

Aunt Amber shrugged. "I can try, but I'm really not very good at that sort of stuff."

It was obvious that Aunt Amber wasn't going to try at all. I couldn't really blame her. Once Aunt Pearl awoke, she would undoubtedly avenge her sister's betrayal of confidence. But there were two people trapped outside. I had to rescue them, but I couldn't rely on my aunts. As usual, they were acting like ten-year-olds. It would be comical if the situation weren't so grave.

"It would have been nice if you had mentioned Pearl's arrangement with Merlinda earlier," Tyler said.

Aunt Amber glanced nervously at her dozing sister. "I wanted to tell you...but Pearl swore me to secrecy. In fact, she made me sign a non-disclosure agreement. That's why I couldn't mention their business arrangement. I don't know all the specifics. Pearl was going to announce it over dinner. Just before Merlinda…" Her voice trailed off as she eyed the hallway.

"Under the circumstances, you still should have said something," I said.

Aunt Amber shook her head as she wiped a tear from her cheek. "Oh, Pearl would have been furious if I had spoiled her surprise. That's also why she invited Brayden to dinner. He promised tax breaks if the Pearl's Charm School head office stayed in Westwick Corners."

"Wait—what? Even Brayden knew all about Aunt Pearl's business plans before we did?" I was so angry that I briefly considered leaving him in the snow globe.

Aunt Amber nodded. "Brayden and Pearl planned to do a joint press release in early January."

I was the only 'press' to speak of in Westwick Corners, and opening a magic school on some far away island was hardly local news. What infuriated me most was that everybody knew but me. If Aunt Amber knew, then so did Mom. Brayden knew, and it stood to reason that Merlinda would have told Dominic. It was like a conspiracy. Everyone knew but Tyler and me. And, quite possibly, Earl.

"Not everyone." Grandma Vi hovered in front of me, interrupting my thoughts. I hated how she always read my mind.

I started to speak but caught myself in time. I didn't want to look like even more of a lunatic in front of Tyler, who couldn't see or hear Grandma Vi.

I refocused on Aunt Amber. "How is a tax break that pits the town against Aunt Pearl 'news'?" I made quote marks with my fingers. "It's really just bad news for the rest of us taxpayers because we have to pay more tax to make up the difference."

I couldn't see how it would benefit the town in any way. Just as I suspected, Aunt Pearl hadn't invited Brayden to our family Christmas Eve dinner out of the goodness of her heart. She had done it for financial reasons.

Aunt Amber shrugged. "Don't ask me. You know I hate all that financial stuff. Makes my head spin. I just did what Pearl told me to."

Tyler's eyes met mine. "That reminds me. Merlinda's arrangement with Pearl wasn't her only significant partnership lately. Merlinda had another one with Dominic."

"Of course. The secret wedding," I said. "Don't you find it odd that as newlyweds, they hadn't discussed details about Merlinda's flight home? If Dominic knew about that, why the surprise visit to Westwick Corners?"

"Yeah," Tyler said. "Considering she would have already left town if her flight hadn't been canceled because of the storm. There's no way he could have known that ahead of time. He also needed to book ahead of time at Christmas."

I nodded. "All the flights in and out of the Shady Creek airport were canceled this morning due to the storm, just as Merlinda's was. There's only one daily flight into Shady Creek. That flight never arrived, so Dominic must have already been in town before today."

Aunt Amber shook her head. "Westwick Corners is far too small. An out of town visitor like Dominic would be noticed. Everybody knows everybody here. And they all gossip too."

"Maybe he stayed in Shady Creek," I said. Dominic's flashy Cadillac rental was a fish out of water amongst the town's pickups and minivans. His tattooed appearance would attract attention too.

I turned to Tyler, but he was already on his cell phone. He said something I couldn't quite make out, then disconnected. He pocketed his phone and turned to us. "It turns out that Dominic's been staying at the Shady Creek Motel 6 for about a week."

"He was already close by but didn't tell Merlinda?" Aunt Amber's eyes widened. "That's not normal newlywed behavior. Why wait to see her?"

"He told me that Aunt Pearl had invited him to surprise Merlinda. Which is really odd that he would have spoken to Aunt Pearl and not Merlinda." I flashed back to Dominic's arrival. How had Aunt Pearl known that Merlinda wouldn't end up catching her flight home?

Unless she had planned something. It struck me as odd that she would even announce the new Vanuatu business venture, let alone invite other people to spend Christmas with us. She was ornery, unpredictable, and secretive. But something had gone wrong because I knew she would never have harmed Merlinda.

At least I didn't think she would. But someone had harmed Merlinda. I felt certain that Aunt Pearl would never kill someone, but I could see her covering up a terrible accident. She never liked to admit she was wrong either. How far would she go to hide the truth?

First, her botched tea, then, the secret arrangement with Brayden, and now, this secret with Dominic. It explained why the two men were at our family celebration. But it was so unlike Aunt Pearl. I kept coming back to the same thing, though. Aunt Pearl never made mistakes with spells or potions. But the most incriminating thing of all was that she never ever extended hospitality to anyone for any reason, inside our family or out. As in never, ever.

Aunt Pearl was guilty of something. I was certain it wasn't murder, though—or was I?

CHAPTER 26

As my mind grappled with what Aunt Pearl was truly capable of, Grandma Vi flitted back and forth in the living room. She was visibly upset.

"Cendrine, how could you even consider such a thing? Pearl would never harm anyone."

I don't know what to think, Grandma. Nobody saw what happened to Merlinda, so I'm looking at all the possibilities. Did you see anything?

Grandma Vi shook her head slowly. "I was too busy feeling sorry for myself while you were all devouring your dinner."

Wait—you can read everyone's mind here, can't you? Whoever killed Merlinda would have been thinking about it.

"That's not how it works, Cen. When I read minds I only hear what I'm focused on. In other words, I have to make an effort to read a mind. With all of you in the same room talking and thinking, it's nigh impossible to pick out one person's thoughts enough to make any sense of it. If only I knew what was about to happen…Sorry, but I've got no hot tips for you."

"But under the right circumstances…" It wasn't too late. Maybe the killer was thinking about the crime right now. All we had to do was get the killer in the same room as Grandma Vi.

Tyler frowned. "Cen, what did you just say?"

"Nothing…uh, maybe it would be a good idea to interview each person in private." I hesitated to call ourselves suspects but technically we all were. Even Tyler in fact. And me too.

Someone still had to get to the bottom of things. Rightly or wrongly, I felt certain that I could rule out my own family members as killers. What I couldn't rule out was whether one of them had caused a tragic accident.

Whatever Aunt Pearl's involvement was, the sooner we cleared that up, the better. If she had messed up her herbal tea, it was best to own up to it. If it was something worse, well, I didn't want to even think about that. My stomach churned at the thought.

Aunt Amber looked worried. "Cen, you're not seriously thinking that Pearl killed Merlinda, are you? I mean, sure, she made a mistake with her tea, but it was an accident."

Aunt Pearl's eyes fluttered open at the mention of her tea. "I told you, Amber, there was absolutely nothing wrong with my tea. We'll never expose the killer if you keep talking nonsense." She yawned and snuggled back into the couch.

I pushed the thought of a killer from my mind and turned to Aunt Pearl. "Tell me more about your secret business opportunity."

Apart from witchcraft, Aunt Pearl's mission in life was pretty much focused on driving as many business people as she could out of town. Yet, now, she was recruiting them. That in itself was a huge red flag.

Aunt Pearl's eyes grew round and she batted her false eyelashes in mock innocence. "What business opportunity? I have no idea what you are talking about."

"Your Pearl's Charm School franchise," I said.

Aunt Pearl gave me a blank stare. "What franchise?"

"Your Vanuatu partnership with Merlinda." Even Aunt Pearl was exploiting Merlinda. "What's in it for you?"

"Oh, that." Aunt Pearl's bony shoulders rose under her green velvet pantsuit as she shook a finger at Aunt Amber. "I knew your loose lips couldn't keep a secret. Look, all I did was give Merlinda free room and board here out of the goodness of my heart. In return, she gave me a share of her Vanuatu business. I refused, but she insisted."

"You kicked me out of my own house only to give my room to a stranger absolutely free?" Grandma Vi's ghostly visage darkened into a deep shade of red. She was furious. "You told me we made money renting it out. How could you betray me like that?"

Grandma Vi now lived with me in a separate dwelling on the property. Our spacious tree house was modern, comfortable, and private--perfect accommodations for a ghost. She had moved in with me at the time we converted our family mansion into a boutique bed and breakfast, long before Merlinda had boarded in Grandma Vi's old room. Grandma Vi's move had been necessary because we couldn't risk her haunting our guests. She still wasn't over it.

"Nobody kicked you out," Aunt Pearl said. "That wasn't the arrangement at all."

"Well, what exactly was the arrangement?" Grandma Vi demanded. "Whatever it was, it's nothing like this. I want restitution. And I want my old room back."

We all ignored her.

"Why would Merlinda start a business on Vanuatu? I thought she wanted to run away from all that." I was frustrated with the ever-changing story. I was also hurt that Grandma Vi disliked being my roommate.

Aunt Amber interrupted. "It's true that Merlinda wanted to leave Vanuatu for good, but Pearl talked her out of it. Pearl wanted Merlinda to capitalize on her talents and profit from it."

Aunt Pearl threw her hands up in the air. "There goes another secret. You sing like a canary, Amber. Such a big mouth."

"So it's true then?" I already knew the answer.

Aunt Amber nodded. "The two of them planned to open a Pearl's Charm School branch on Vanuatu."

That made no sense. The one and only operating branch of Pearl's Charm School was barely solvent with one student. Replicating that business model on some far-away island seemed financially disastrous. On the other hand, Merlinda was something of a supernatural workhorse, at least according to the cargo cult magic stories. Maybe Aunt Pearl planned to take advantage of her too.

"Stop butting in, Amber," Aunt Pearl said. "I can speak for myself."

"Well then, why don't you?" Aunt Amber asked sweetly. She was clearly pleased at getting her sister all riled up.

Aunt Pearl was wide awake by now. "Nice try, but I won't be tricked into revealing my business secrets. I'll lose my competitive edge."

Aunt Amber shrugged. "I guess it's up to me then. Pearl planned to join Merlinda in Vanuatu after Christmas to set up shop. She would get everything rolling in exchange for a percentage of the fees. Merlinda was her protégé."

"Don't talk about me like I'm not even here," Aunt Pearl protested. "Half of what you're saying isn't even true."

"Which parts exactly?" Tyler asked.

Aunt Pearl shrugged. "What does it matter?"

Aunt Amber shook her head in disappointment. "This is really serious, Pearl. I waited for you to say something, to own up to it. But you never did."

"Never will, either. I want a lawyer." Aunt Pearl fidgeted on the sofa, restless. The spell was completely worn off now.

I frowned. "If Merlinda was worried about her father trying to take advantage of her supernatural talents, wouldn't the new business just antagonize him?"

"That's where Pearl comes in," Aunt Amber said. "Two witches are better than one, and her father would be powerless to stop them. They would operate as Pearl's Charm School together at first, with Merlinda taking over in time. The islanders would see that Merlinda held the magic of the cargo cult, not her father or anyone else. That's the one thing that would free her from his grip. Pearl would be her backup in case she got backlash from her father."

Aunt Pearl could be very persuasive. Maybe Merlinda had felt pressured to go along with her plan. "I don't get it. Merlinda wanted to stop the John Frum cargo cult charade. This just perpetuates it."

Aunt Amber shrugged. "Pearl convinced Merlinda that she could showcase her talents, and maybe even encourage some of the locals to develop their own supernatural talents. Pearl can make a witch out of pretty much anyone. As long as they apply themselves."

Aunt Pearl beamed at the compliment. "Told you, Cen."

I rolled my eyes at the dig. I was sick and tired of being called a lousy witch.

Aunt Amber patted my shoulder. "Don't take it too personally, Cen. Pearl saw both Merlinda's potential and a huge market opportunity. She figured that if all of the believers in the cargo cult applied themselves, they wouldn't be taken advantage of. With a few simple spells, she felt she could entice them into enrolling in her school."

"You mean, bewitch them into enrolling. That's cheating." It sounded like more trouble than it was worth, not to mention against WICCA rules. But if Aunt Pearl was anything, she was an opportunist.

"But if the other islanders aren't witches, how can they practice witchcraft?" Grandma Vi asked. "How is that even possible?"

Aunt Pearl grinned. "It's all in the secret sauce. Anything's possible when you believe in yourself."

This was just wrong, and I had to say so. "Oh, I get it. You're going to prey on these poor souls and promise the impossible. You think that since they believe in the cargo cult and John Frum, you can just take their tuition money and convince them that they can actually become witches."

"Geez, Cen. You make it sound so callous."

"Well, it is. You'll do anything for a buck."

"Pretty much," Aunt Pearl smiled. "Or a vatu. That's the currency in Vanuatu."

<h1 style="text-align:center">CHAPTER 27</h1>

It was painfully obvious by now that no one was going to help me get Brayden and Gail back. It was small consolation to know that Aunt Amber and Grandma Vi weren't much better at witchcraft than I was. Now, I had no one to look up to. Well, almost no one.

Mom was much more accomplished than I was, but she limited herself to only a dozen or so spells. I had probably inherited my lack of commitment from her. The only real possibility was Aunt Pearl, but she had made it clear that I had to do it myself. Brayden and Gail's future, or lack thereof, rested solely in my hands.

My spell book was back at my treehouse, but walking through the snowdrifts to retrieve it would take too long. Anything could go wrong while Brayden and Gail were stuck in limbo, and I couldn't risk that.

Suddenly, I remembered that Mom's spell book was in the house. I raced into the kitchen and rummaged through the messy bottom drawer of the desk where Mom kept her WICCA spell book. I pulled it out. It was dusty, probably because Mom rarely referred to it these days. She focused mostly on herbal remedies that she knew by heart.

The worn leather cover felt reassuring against my palm as I opened the book. I thumbed through the thin vellum pages and soon found the Transport spell and its reversal spell. The familiar words came back to me as I read the first line.

As I read more, I stumbled. The wording in Mom's older edition was slightly different than what I had read in my own spell book. Not by much, but enough to make me wonder. Were the text changes made just to modernize, or was there a problem with the older version?

I always followed my spells to the letter and still had trouble pulling them off. What if the wording differences in the older version meant they no longer worked? Or worse, what if they were harmful? One small mistake could have very serious consequences for Brayden and Gail.

In the end, it was a chance I had to take. I had no other options. I held the book open and ran back outside to the front porch. I had to be completely focused on the task at hand without distraction from my aunts or anyone else. I also couldn't risk their interference. That gave me only a minute or so before somebody came outside to see what I was doing, and I needed the solitude to concentrate.

I reread the page, focusing my sights on Brayden and Gail in the snow globe on the lawn. They no longer banged on the glass. Instead, they barely moved as they huddled together for warmth.

I had to make this work.

I read the words several times until I had them committed to memory. Then I channeled all my energies to the glass globe on the lawn and recited the words:

COME BACK, come back,
  Return to me,
  From whence you came,
  And you will be free,

· · ·

Tap-a-tap-tap
  On the glass
  Take the steps
  And bring yourself back.

THE SPELL WAS short and sweet, much simpler than I had assumed it would be. It was the opposite of the original transport spell. All I had to do was speak clearly and visualize Brayden and Gail.

But nothing happened.

I repeated the spell a half-dozen times.

Nothing.

Was it different because they were inside a glass globe? Were there other kinds of globes? I hadn't the foggiest idea. I flashed back to my own glass snow globe imprisonment. I couldn't remember exactly how I had escaped, but I had somehow made it back. So would Brayden and Gail. I could do this.

According to Aunt Amber, Aunt Pearl had forgotten the last sentence of the spell she had used on me. I looked down at my book and reread the last line. That line at least was identical to the one I remembered from my own spell book. It hadn't seemed to matter that Aunt Amber had interrupted and spoken the last line of Aunt Pearl's spell. It seemed that anyone could voice the words...whether it was one witch or two. There had to be another reason why my spell wasn't working and why I couldn't bring them back.

The last thing I remembered about my snow globe prison was a low rumbling sound, the reindeer pawing at the ground, and then the glass shattering just as I was finally freed.

Sheer force could be another way to break the spell. If I couldn't conjure it, maybe I could come up with something similar. I just needed enough power to break the glass without harming Brayden and Gail, and if I kept it concentrated under the globe, I could break them out.

I leaned against the house as I flipped through Mom's spell book with half-frozen fingers. There were several spells that could work in a pinch: an earthquake spell, and an apocalypse spell. Workable, but a little drastic. The widespread catastrophic destruction would no doubt annihilate us all. Aside from that, even more could go wrong, especially in my hands.

That brought me back to the transport reversal spell. I recited the spell again, careful to speak slowly and clearly.

Nothing.

Like Einstein said, repeating the same thing over and over again and expecting a different result was insanity.

I did it out of sheer desperation because I didn't know what else to do.

I had just turned to go back inside when the force of the blast knocked me off my feet. I fell backward and slipped on the edge of the ice-covered front porch. Then everything went dark.

CHAPTER 28

I opened my eyes and stared into the worried gaze of Tyler. He squeezed my hand. "Cen, what happened? Brayden found you on the front porch. You were knocked out cold."

Brayden? If he was out of the globe, then my spell had worked! Maybe the magnetic pull of Merlinda's globe had waned. Or, perhaps I had found my witch calling after all. Whatever it was, I was both relieved and proud.

"I can't remember..." I was propped up with pillows on the living room sofa and couldn't remember how I got there. My last memory was standing outside on the porch reciting the spell. Everything after that was a blank. I sat up straight and scanned the room.

Mom, Aunt Pearl, and Aunt Amber stood in the hall doorway.

Brayden sat in the overstuffed chair by the hearth. He smiled, a look of relief on his face. "How ya doing, Cen? You gave me quite a scare."

From the looks of it, Brayden had no memory of the snow globe.

Aunt Pearl smiled. "Cendrine West! You put on quite a show when you apply yourself. See what you can do with a little effort?"

I nodded. I massaged my forehead and recalled the spell. All I recalled was reciting the last line from Mom's spell book. Mom's book! I glanced around me but didn't see it anywhere. I must have left it out on the porch. No doubt it was wet and damaged by now. I bolted upright and scrambled to my feet. "I have to get the book."

"Relax, Cen." Mom tapped her fingers on her spell book. "I've got it right here. Nothing to worry about."

"Where's everybody else?" I really meant Gail, but I didn't want to single her out.

"If you're looking for little 'ol me, I'm right here," Grandma Vi called out from above my head. "Whew! That was a close call. You almost got me too. Did you miss me?"

I tilted my head slightly, just enough for her to notice.

She flitted down beside me and hovered just above the armrest. "Did I ever tell you that you're my favorite granddaughter?"

I'm your only granddaughter.

Tyler smiled. "You really don't remember anything, Cen? You found Brayden and Gail almost frozen to death outside. A few more minutes and they would have both been frostbitten."

Grandma Vi gave an exaggerated shiver. "Oh my! You really saved the day, Cendrine."

Gail suddenly reappeared at the mention of her name. She had changed out of her wet clothes and showered, a towel wrapped around her head. She also wore Mom's bathrobe. "Got anything I can wear?"

Everybody turned to me.

I shook my head. "Sorry, but all my stuff is back at my treehouse. I guess you'll just have to wait for your stuff to dry." I was secretly relieved and almost gleeful that her sequined miniskirt and leather jacket couldn't just be tossed in the dryer.

She couldn't exactly go on the run in Mom's housecoat either. Which was good because I had a lot of unanswered questions.

Aunt Amber had one too.

"Did you know that pomegranate in French is grenade?" Aunt Amber asked.

I wasn't sure if she was referring to me blowing apart Merlinda's globe or something else, but we were in danger of getting sidetracked. "What does that have to be with anything, Aunt Amber?"

She shrugged. "Oh, nothing. Or, maybe everything. I get the feeling that things are about to blow up."

I had no idea what Aunt Amber was getting at, but I knew something else. I had busted Brayden and Gail out of their prison, and I wanted something in return. Granted, I had trapped them in the glass globe in the first place. Still, things could have been much worse if I hadn't ended up rescuing them.

Gail looked up from towel-drying her hair. "Damn right things aren't what they seem. Take Merlinda for instance. Why was everyone in such awe of her? She was no angel."

The kitchen door slammed followed by heavy footsteps. Dominic appeared in the dining room doorway. He was wet and disheveled like he had been outside. "Hey—watch what you're saying about Merlinda, Have some respect. She's the victim here."

"Hardly," Gail scoffed. "Just a poor little rich girl who cried when she didn't get what she wanted."

I looked him up and down and wondered if Aunt Pearl had something to do with his messy appearance. "What happened to you?"

Dominic ignored me. He scowled at Gail. "You wouldn't know. You never even gave Merlinda a chance."

Tyler and I exchanged glances. What on earth were they talking about? The angry undercurrent between Gail and Dominic struck me as odd for two people who had just met.

Gail opened her mouth to speak but thought better of it.

"That right there is the bomb." Aunt Amber smiled. "Touché."

CHAPTER 29

"You two know each other, don't you?" I looked first at Gail and then Dominic.

Gail looked away and towel-dried her hair with increased frenzy.

Her enraged reaction told me I had hit a nerve. Dominic and Gail knew each other all right, and we had just unmasked them. Yet another secret exposed.

"Yeah, we know each other,' Dominic said softly. "I wish now that we didn't."

Brayden's eyes widened in shock. "How could you guys know each other? Dominic just flew in from Vanuatu, and you live in Shady Creek…"

Gail shrugged, a smug expression on her face.

Brayden searched Gail's face for an answer. "You lied to me."

Gail sniffed. "I didn't lie. I didn't say anything because I thought you'd get mad."

"Why would I be mad?" Brayden looked confused as he glanced back and forth between Gail and Dominic. Realization slowly dawned that their relationship had probably been romantic, not platonic.

Gail grabbed Brayden's hand and pulled him close. "I can explain, Bray. Dominic and I used to see each other a long, long time ago before he moved to Vanuatu. But you're the one I'm with now, and that's all that matters."

Brayden's mouth dropped open. "But why hide that from me? What's going on, Gail?"

"I didn't hide anything from you. You just never asked," Gail replied sweetly.

Brayden looked confused. "B-but why would I ask in the first place? You both acted like you just met for the first time."

Gail dismissed Brayden with a wave of her hand. "You don't need to know every single detail of my life, Brayden. But since I've got nothing to hide...Dominic and I dated for a few months. I never mentioned it because I knew you'd get jealous. Just like you are right now."

Brayden had many faults but jealousy wasn't one of them. As an ignored ex-girlfriend, I knew that firsthand. He focused on himself too much to notice things like that. Like, not even at all. I really felt sorry for him, though. He didn't deserve the treatment Gail was dishing out.

"Uh, yeah, that's right." Dominic looked visibly relieved. He turned to Brayden. "It was such a long time ago. You got a problem with that?"

Brayden swallowed hard as a flicker of doubt flashed across his face. "Uh...I guess not. Just friends now, right?"

"Yeah," Dominic said. "No big deal."

I flashed back to dinner and Gail's enraged expression over Merlinda. People got jealous all the time, but there was something more going on with her. Something beyond envy. Something sinister, in fact. Even wrapped in Mom's fluffy housecoat she looked scary. Something told me not to turn my back on her.

"I'll talk to any man I want, Brayden," Gail said. "You don't own me, so stop acting so controlling." She spoke to Brayden but focused her angry glare on Dominic.

"I'm not…I just thought you would have said something…" Brayden's hurt expression said it all. He had been completely blindsided by Gail's revelation. "I mean, we're spending Christmas together after all."

I turned to Gail. "You two dated each other? When?"

"It's really none of your business, Cendrine," Gail snapped.

Brayden crossed his arms. "Well, it's definitely my business. If there's nothing between you and Dominic, then why hide it? What's going on, Gail?"

Gail swore under her breath but didn't elaborate further.

I turned to Gail. "I think your relationship with Dominic is much more recent than you're letting on. Running into each other here is too much of a coincidence. Dating Brayden was just a ruse to invite yourself to our Christmas Eve dinner."

"I told Brayden to bring a date. I just never expected him to bring a stalker," Aunt Pearl said.

I glared at Aunt Pearl.

"Is what Cen is saying true?" Brayden turned to Gail.

Gail remained silent.

Dominic cleared his throat and stared awkwardly at the floor.

No answer was answer enough.

Everything clicked into place and I knew. "Admit it, Gail. You were jealous of Merlinda. It wasn't Brayden's wandering eye, though. It was Dominic's relationship with Merlinda that enraged you."

"Why would I be jealous of her? I don't care who Dominic dates." Gail's casual dismissal contrasted with her angry expression. She spat out her words like poison.

"Oh, but you do care," I said. "You manipulated Brayden into dating you. Admit it, Gail. Your whirlwind romance was just a ploy to get to Dominic and Merlinda."

"Why would I do that? I have a boyfriend." Gail glanced at Brayden for reassurance.

"I'm not so sure anymore," Brayden said. "You're still not telling me everything, I can tell. I don't like being used."

Brash and out of control Gail was such an unlikely match for staid, social-climbing Brayden. Though Brayden had brought Gail to dinner to make me jealous, he wasn't the type to use people. He had fallen victim to Gail's lies and manipulation instead.

Brayden and Gail weren't the only oddball couple. Dominic seemed wrong for Merlinda too, not that I had known Merlinda all that well in the first place. Gail and Dominic, on the other hand, made perfect sense. In fact, they deserved each other. The puzzle pieces all fit together.

"I can explain everything, Bray." Gail grabbed Brayden's hand. "Let's go somewhere quiet and talk."

Brayden snatched his hand away. "No. I've seen enough."

Dominic turned to Gail. "Okay, if Brayden's breaking things off, then let's talk. We've got a lot of catching up to do."

Unbelievable. In the wake of Merlinda's sudden death, Dominic wanted to patch things up with Gail.

Gail scowled at Dominic. "You jerk—I've got nothing to say to you. I thought I knew you. Turns out that I really don't know you at all."

Dominic raised his right hand. "Gail, I can explain—"

Any pretense of strangers was gone.

Gail covered her ears. "Save it for someone who cares."

"I do care." Dominic swallowed hard. "I just never expected this..."

"You betrayed me, Dom. I thought we had a future together." Her voice broke and her lower lip trembled. She was close to tears, crumbling beneath her tough exterior.

Brayden shook his head. "I don't believe this. I feel like such an idiot."

"Well, you are one for bringing that woman." Grandma Vi floated above Brayden's head.

"You got that right," Aunt Pearl said.

Dominic sighed. "You might as well know because you'll find out sooner or later. Even if Gail won't admit it. She's from Vanuatu too."

Gail waved her hand in dismissal. "That's crazy. I have no idea what he's talking about."

"Wait—what?" Brayden's brows furrowed together in confusion. He turned to Gail. "If you're from Vanuatu, why don't you have an accent?"

"She's a transplanted American, just like me," Dominic said. "We both worked for the dive shop at Merlinda's family's hotel."

Their coupledom was obvious in hindsight. They were around the same age. Both were a little pushy and rough around the edges. Their relationship hadn't occurred to me until now because they were already matched—or perhaps mismatched—with other people.

"You were played, Brayden," Aunt Pearl said. "You're just too dumb to figure out that Gail used you. She was never interested in you at all. You're too dull."

"Aunt Pearl!" I said. Her blunt honesty was almost as bad as her habitual lies.

"But...but—" Brayden's face flushed crimson.

I felt a twinge of sympathy for my ex-fiancé. Brayden wasn't dumb. He was just too self-absorbed to have seen Gail for what she really was: a cold and calculating manipulator using him to get what she wanted.

Hurt was written all over Brayden's face. For the first time in a long time he needed us, and I wasn't going to let him down.

I wanted to give him a hug.

But instead, I dished out some good old-fashioned witchcraft.

Revenge is a dish best served cold.

CHAPTER 30

My frozen spell had worked. Maybe a little too well in fact, since I had only meant to freeze Gail and Dominic, not Brayden too. Brayden was collateral damage because he was standing too close to Gail when I executed my spell.

Oops. I did it again.

Mom held onto Aunt Amber for support. "Whew! That was close, Cen. You almost caught us up in your spell too. Give us a warning next time."

"Sorry, Mom. I guess I got caught up in the moment." Truth be told, I never expected my spell to work in the first place. Usually they didn't because I always missed one or two important details. Today was different. I was on a roll, witch-wise.

"Well done, Cen!" Aunt Pearl clapped her hands together. "There's hope for you yet."

I beamed at the backhanded compliment as I studied our three unconscious guests. I had used a frozen spell on Gail, Dominic, and Brayden as a way to defuse the situation. Their love triangle threatened to derail our investigation just as we were getting to the bottom of things. The last thing we needed was another death on our hands.

My spell was nowhere near as robust as Aunt Pearl's spells, but it was strong enough to allow us a few minutes to talk amongst ourselves. Spellcasting wasn't all that hard once you got the hang of it. I resolved to devote more time and focus to my craft. Practice makes perfect. It would be my New Year's resolution.

Tyler frowned. "I hope you have a plan, Cen."

"Of course," I lied. My magic on the fly had frozen the love triangle and given us a few minutes to talk. Beyond that, I had no clue on what to do next.

Earl entered the room and stopped abruptly at the sight of our three temporarily frozen guests. He stepped back, then tripped on the throw rug and stumbled backwards

Tyler caught him just in time and steadied him.

"Yikes! What the heck's going on here?" Earl's voice jumped a couple of octaves. "I better not be next!"

Tyler shook his head. "Expect the unexpected, Earl. You should know that about the West women by now."

Aunt Pearl waved an arm in dismissal. "Don't listen to him, Earl. You've got nothing to worry about. You know I'll always protect—" She stopped mid-sentence once she saw us all staring at her.

Aunt Amber smacked her lips together in an air kiss. "Aww... Pearl's so sweet on you, Earl. What's your secret? I've just never seen her like this with anybody before."

"Amber, cut that out!" Aunt Pearl blushed.

Earl was embarrassed too. His flushed face blended into his red flannel shirt. He ignored Aunt Amber's question and changed the subject. He pointed to my three temporary casualties slumped together on the floor. "What's wrong with them?"

"Uh...nothing's wrong." I hastily made up a story to explain our comatose guests. "They're having a nap while we figure things out."

"You mean like what happened to Merlinda?" Surely, Earl had been around Aunt Pearl long enough to have more than just an inkling of her witchy powers, and by extension, mine. There was just so much about our family that defied explanation.

Earl was laid-back, but he was smart too. Which made his attraction to Aunt Pearl all the more mysterious. Maybe it was an attraction of intellects. It couldn't possibly be her sunny personality.

I nodded. "Yes. It should just take a few minutes."

Aunt Pearl smiled brightly. "What Cen really means is that we're playing a game to see who can play dead the longest. You missed it when you left the room."

Aunt Amber sucked in her breath. "Really bad word choice, Pearl."

Aunt Pearl rolled her eyes. "You know what I mean."

We were really delaying the inevitable because Aunt Pearl's games had to come full circle back to the truth. And the truth was that a killer was still amongst us.

Earl wasn't buying Aunt Pearl's game nonsense, either. He shrugged and walked toward the window. "Sounds a bit sedate for you, Pearl. I'm thinking of heading home. The storm's let up now, and the last few hours have been a little much for my ticker. I can't afford a heart attack."

"Nobody's going anywhere," Tyler said. "Especially not you, Earl. I might need your help."

"Now Earl…" Aunt Pearl blushed, her normally cranky voice smooth as honey. "For once I agree with the sheriff. You'll just be bored at home. You know how you like to keep busy. Just stay…I promise I'll make it worth your while."

"I don't know…" Earl stared wistfully out the window. "I'm feeling kind of tired. You people exhaust me sometimes."

Aunt Pearl stamped her foot, her sunny disposition of moments earlier gone. "You can't leave now. I have so much planned, and we've barely even started our Christmas celebrations."

"That's what scares me." Earl waved his arm in the direction of our three captives. "You can't just knock people out whenever you feel like it."

"Cen did that, not me. It will take her forever to fix it, though. As usual, I've got to make things right." Aunt Pearl waved her arms and muttered under her breath.

I started to protest, but it was too late.

Dominic's eyes fluttered open. Then Brayden awoke, followed by Gail seconds later.

"See, Earl? No harm done." Aunt Pearl squeezed Earl's arm. "Just stay awhile longer, and help me get this show on the road. You won't regret it."

Aunt Pearl certainly had no regrets. Exactly what I was afraid of.

CHAPTER 31

Our three groggy guests scrambled to their feet. They were tired, dazed, and confused. They also looked a lot worse for wear than they had earlier.

Brayden shuffled over to the sofa and collapsed. He rubbed his temples. "I've got a pounding headache. I wish I had just stayed home."

I put the spell back on Brayden to spare him more misery, both headache-wise and Gail-wise. Within seconds he was fast asleep.

"Yeah, well, I'm going home. Back to Vanuatu." Dominic turned to Gail. "Want a ride back to Shady Creek? The weather's improved, so the roads should be passable now. We'll wait for the airport to re-open and catch the next flight out."

I glanced outside and noticed that Dominic's Escalade was once again parked in the driveway.

"Over my dead body, sonny," Aunt Pearl said.

Gail snorted. "That can be arranged, old lady."

Tyler stepped between Gail and Aunt Pearl and dangled Dominic's car keys. "Nobody's going anywhere until I say so. And that won't be happening until we know what happened to Merlinda. So start talking."

"Yeah, that's right." Earl stood behind Tyler. "You're all staying put right here."

Gail fumbled in her purse for her cell phone. "What is wrong with you people? You can't keep us here. I'm calling the cops."

"No need. Sheriff Gates is right here," Aunt Amber said sweetly.

"I meant the real cops. This is a joke. The sheriff hasn't done anything to keep us safe," Gail said. "I don't know what you crazy people are up to, but I'm not going to stay here and suffer the same fate as Merlinda."

Dominic rubbed his head. "Me neither."

Gail gasped and clutched her stomach. "Wait a minute—I think somebody poisoned me too. It's that Christmas cake. Or, maybe it's the tea…Whatever it is, I feel terrible."

"Who are you accusing—" Aunt Pearl stopped mid-sentence. "Oh no, you don't. You're trying to frame Ruby and me!"

Aunt Amber grabbed Aunt Pearl from behind and placed a hand over her mouth.

Dominic leaned against the wall for support. "I'm feeling kind of sick myself."

Gail turned to Dominic. "We're both going to die, and it's all your fault. If you had just done what you were supposed to do, I wouldn't be here right now."

"Whatever. I'm done arguing with you." Dominic slumped down into a sitting position against the wall.

"Quit stalling," Tyler said. "It only makes things worse for you both in the end. You two are still hiding something, and I want to know what it is."

"Yeah--spill the beans," Aunt Pearl demanded. "Tell us what you did to Merlinda."

Dominic held his hands up, palms out in protest. "I didn't do anything to Merlinda, I swear. I am not taking the fall for this. I told Gail that I couldn't go through with it, but she wouldn't listen. This isn't what it looks like. I can explain everything."

"The hell you will." Gail grabbed Merlinda's tropical snow globe from the tree and hurled it at Dominic. "You told me that it was only work. That getting close to Merlinda was all part of the master plan. Liar!"

"Gail, I'm sorry I didn't mean to—" Dominic ducked as the glass snow globe flew through the air.

Fortunately, Gail's aim was off. I lunged into the line of fire and outstretched my arm to catch the glass globe. The globe barely glowed now that its creator was forever gone. It still felt wrong for whatever remained to end as shattered glass.

My fingers connected but only just barely. I balanced precariously on one foot and balanced the globe with one hand. It was too big to grasp with my palm. It rolled down my forearm like a bowling ball instead. The glass orb hit my chest, throwing me off balance.

I suspected Merlinda's globe held even more powers than what I had already witnessed, but I had no desire to test my theory. Every witch created spells a little differently. Some even booby-trapped spells to prevent tampering by other witches. Whether Merlinda had protected the globe in some way other than the magnetic repellent I had no idea. Dropping the glass globe was out of the question, though.

I sighed in relief once I had the globe firmly within my grasp. I pressed it safely against my stomach and held it close as I regained my balance.

Gail picked up an empty wineglass and threw it at Dominic. This time she hit her target. "You jerk! You said Merlinda would make us rich. Instead, you got greedy and betrayed me. You were supposed to kill her, not marry her!"

Dominic held out his arms, palms out in surrender. "She's dead, isn't she? You got what you wanted." His voice broke as he struggled to contain his emotions.

"You fell in love with Merlinda." Aunt Pearl looked knowingly at Dominic. Her voice broke. "Yet, you killed her anyway. How could you?"

"I-I didn't kill her, I swear. I was supposed to kidnap her, not kill her. But I couldn't even manage that. I backed out because I loved her. I just couldn't do it."

"Liar," Gail hissed. "You're incapable of love. You got greedy and decided to cut me out of the deal. That's why you never returned my messages. You left me stuck working at the dive shop handling everything, waiting for you. You never even called once to ask how I was doing. Now I know why. Instead of kidnapping Merlinda, you've been romancing her all this time. You thought you could marry rich and inherit everything. Well, you killed the golden goose. I hope you rot in jail, you two-timing loser!"

CHAPTER 32

Brayden snored loudly on the sofa, oblivious to the Gail versus Dominic standoff that unfolded before us. The rest of us formed a loose semi-circle around Gail and Dominic. They faced each other as if they were about to duel to the death.

Dominic was either a criminal with no conscience or a grieving husband whose actions had gotten his wife killed in the first place. Either way, I felt no pity. He had been caught red-handed and seemed eager to incriminate Gail and shift the blame off himself.

Dominic sighed. "We had planned to kidnap Merlinda and demand a ransom from her father. Once that happened, we would send a proof of life video showing Merlinda pleading for help. We knew Merlinda's father would pay the ransom because he needed Merlinda and her supernatural powers back on Vanuatu. He needed her to conjure up more cargo. His whole John Frum scheme depended on it."

"Except you couldn't even do that right," Gail said. "When you didn't call, I had to come here to make sure you finished the job. Then I find out that you've hooked up with her instead. We planned everything together, Dom. How could you do this to me?"

"I told you I couldn't go through with it, but you just wouldn't listen." Dominic turned to Tyler, his voice breaking as tears streamed down his face. "I broke things off with Gail a while ago, so it's not like I'm cheating on her now."

Aunt Pearl snorted. "How thoughtful of you. You're gonna get what's coming to you, sonny."

I moved beside Aunt Pearl, ready to tackle her if she made a move toward Dominic. I really hoped it wouldn't come to that. "Aunt Pearl…"

"You threatening me, Pearl?" Dominic said. "I wouldn't do that if I were you. I know stuff about you too."

"You're bluffing, sonny," Aunt Pearl said. "You can't have anything on me. I haven't done anything wrong."

"Except maybe the tea," Aunt Amber interjected. "Even you make mistakes, Pearl."

"Cut it out, Amber," Aunt Pearl snapped. "You're not helping."

Aunt Amber shook her head. "Blackmailing Pearl is asking for trouble, young man. You have no idea what she's capable of."

I tapped Aunt Pearl's arm. "You've said enough for now. Let Tyler handle this." Sidetracking the conversation could ruin any chance of a confession.

"Don't tell me to shut up, Cen. Dominic deserves a piece of my mind. And maybe a piece of something else."

"No, Aunt Pearl…" I protested.

Dominic held his arms up in surrender. "You're right. I deserve whatever I have coming to me. For lying and stuff. But not for Merlinda's death. I would never hurt her. I know it looks bad, but I swear I had nothing to do with her death. It's all a horrible accident."

Gail glared at Dominic. "Liar. I had no idea what was going on until tonight when I saw you two together. You married her to cut me out of the deal. Marriage was the ultimate way to harness her powers and make yourself rich in the process. Well, that's not going to happen now, is it?"

"That makes no sense," Dominic said. "Merlinda is worth much less dead than she was alive. Besides, I loved her. I would never have taken advantage of her like that."

I was convinced that Gail hadn't concocted the plan alone without Dominic's involvement. Whether or not he had ultimately backed out, he had been in on the scheme from the beginning.

"Well, I'm not taking the fall for you," Gail snapped. "You're just as responsible as I am."

Dominic wagged his finger at Gail. "Ah-ha! You admit you killed her!"

Gail's eyes narrowed. "Of course not! I'm not admitting anything. I know one thing about you, Dominic. You have a backup plan. I bet you insured that poor girl to the hilt."

Aunt Pearl snorted. "Ooh, so now Merlinda's a poor girl? You never thought that when you killed her."

"Stay out of this, Pearl." Tyler stepped in front of Aunt Pearl and waved her away. He turned to Dominic. "Keep talking."

"I'll admit that we—I mean me—planned on getting close to Merlinda," Dominic said. "The plan was to gain her trust and then kidnap her. That was impossible on Vanuatu. I was outside of her social circle with no way in, no way to get to know her.

"So, back when Merlinda first left Vanuatu for her first semester at Pearl's Charm School, I caught the same flight out. I bribed the airline for a seat next to her and charmed her enough to go out with me. I told her I was an entrepreneur with business in the U.S. But I had to eventually return to Vanuatu and my job at the dive shop while she was going to school here in Westwick Corners. That's how we first started dating. We had a long distance relationship ever since."

Gail scowled. "You dragged everything on so long that I got sick and tired of all your excuses. You just wanted to keep seeing Merlinda when she returned home on semester breaks."

"Our long-distance relationship wasn't enough for me, and Merlinda felt the same way. We secretly got married in Vanuatu during one of her semester breaks."

Gail gasped. "You got married on Vanuatu? Right under my nose? How could you do that to me, Dominic?"

"He couldn't exactly invite you to the wedding." Aunt Amber giggled.

Dominic ignored her, seemingly intent on spilling the rest of his confession now. "We kept our marriage secret, and I stalled Gail. I wasn't about to kidnap my own wife."

Gail snorted. "You didn't need to after cutting me out of the action. You got rich overnight."

Dominic glared at Gail. "Everything came to a head when Merlinda's father found out about the marriage. She had to choose: me or Vanuatu. And I had to choose between Merlinda and Gail's plan."

"Oh, so it's my plan now?" Gail's face reddened. "We were in this together, Dom. Don't try to get out of it. I'm not taking the fall for you."

Dominic sighed, exhaustion showing on his face. "I told Gail no, but she wouldn't hear of it. So, I stalled as long as I could, figuring Merlinda was at least safe here at school. Then Gail said we couldn't wait any longer. That's what brought me here. But I couldn't go through with it."

"Liar," Gail said. "You killed her."

Dominic shook his head. "No. I only ever considered the kidnapping."

Aunt Amber let out a low whistle. "How do you kidnap your own wife? I've never heard of that before. You don't sound all that innocent to me."

"It became necessary for her own protection. To save her from something worse." Dominic let out a heavy sigh. "I really don't know what I was planning. I thought maybe we could both disappear and make a fresh start somewhere. I never expected this."

Tyler waved his arm at all of us. "Showing up for dinner is a strange way to abduct someone. All of us are witnesses. Unless the impromptu visit was all part of the plan. Play the loving husband on a surprise visit, and cut Gail out of the picture."

Dominic nodded slowly. "I guess that part is true. You can lock me up for that. But I didn't kill her."

CHAPTER 33

"Dominic makes it sound like I forced him into kidnapping Merlinda, but that's just not true," Gail said. "He had already demanded $50,000 from Merlinda's father in a ransom letter. Her father would have paid too. Fifty grand is small change compared to what her father earned off Merlinda's spells. He needed her to work her magic."

I turned to Dominic. "Is that true?"

Gail held up her cell phone. "I have a photo of the ransom note right here."

Dominic waved his hands in protest. "I'll admit to the ransom note, but I never ended up sending it. I sure as hell didn't kill Merlinda. I loved her."

"Yeah, sure," Gail snorted. "Just like you said you loved me. Maybe we can still work something out, though. Merlinda's no more, but we can sure put these witchy worker bees to good use."

"Like hell you will." Aunt Pearl glared at Gail. "You better hope we don't do some more work on you."

Aunt Amber's mouth dropped open as she looked first at Aunt

Pearl, then Mom and me. "Wait a minute, Gail—you know we're witches? Who told her?"

As if that was the most pressing thing on all our minds.

As if we hadn't been dancing around the whole witchcraft issue all night with talk of Merlinda's cargo cult and everything else.

"Of course I knew!" Gail said. "You're all so obvious about it. You really think you're so smart, that nobody knows about your 'special sauce'?" She made quote marks with her fingers. "Of course I knew about Merlinda conjuring stuff up. Just like you people making stuff up. That was the whole point of Project John Frum. Only now, I need a Merlinda replacement. If you want in on the action, I can make it worth your while."

"We're not making stuff—" I stopped mid-sentence.

Gail pulled a gun from her purse and pointed it at me. "I think I just found us a new business opportunity, Dom. Grab the old ladies while I deal with this one. We'll start our own cargo cult right here in Westwick Corners."

"You're no match for the Westwick witches, missy!" Aunt Pearl suddenly sprung up between us and, with surprising force, pushed Gail into a chair that had mysteriously appeared behind her. Within seconds invisible hands bound Gail's hands and feet and tied them to the chair with a magically appearing rope.

Aunt Pearl wiped her hands together as if she had just completed an unpleasant task. "I guess you aren't as smart as you think you are."

Gail scowled. "No—I'm smarter than all of you combined. You're all so busy thinking how wonderful you are. In reality, you're all so self-absorbed that you don't even notice other people."

"Or their dirty tricks." Aunt Amber sighed. "I certainly never expected a murder right under my nose. I don't see how that makes me self-absorbed, though."

Gail rolled her eyes. "You're so focused on trivial things that you're completely missing the big picture."

"Quit changing the subject, Gail," Aunt Pearl snapped. "It's not as easy as it looks, you know. Poor Merlinda had to conjure up all kinds of stuff in advance to feed the demands of the cargo cult scam. She had to come home every semester break and work day and night to rebuild inventory; enough to last while she was away at school. And she did it all under duress. That's something you could never do."

Mom nodded. "That girl had to conjure up all that cargo like a supernatural assembly line. I don't get it, though. Her talents made her worth more alive than dead."

"Exactly. To all but one person, that is." I pointed to Gail. "You're the one who benefits the most from her death. Even without the ransom, you needed to exact revenge on Merlinda for stealing Dominic away. You killed her. Not for money but for love."

"Don't be ridiculous," Gail said. "It was Dominic. He got a big fat insurance policy on Merlinda's life. He killed her."

"How much was the policy, Dominic?" Tyler asked.

"It's nothing like it sounds. Merlinda and I both got life insurance because that's what married couples do. You make it sound like I had a price on her head or something. I lost a lot more than I gained. I lost the love of my life." Dominic broke down in sobs.

"Oh, cry me a river," Aunt Pearl said. "Merlinda told me all about you and your manipulation. She was getting ready to leave you for good. You and Gail are like two peas in a pod."

Gail snorted. "See? Dominic killed her to stop her from leaving."

Brayden stirred on the sofa. He slowly opened one eye, then the other.

"Deflecting the blame doesn't work, Gail." I held up the empty bottle of Gail's gas station wine. "You put something in the wine."

Gail shook her head. "Everybody had some wine, but only Merlinda got sick."

"That's not true," I said. "Only you, Brayden, and Merlinda drank white wine, the kind you brought."

"That's ridiculous," Gail said. "I drank the wine, and I'm still here. So did Brayden."

I shook my head. "No. You spilled Brayden's wineglass before he had a chance to take a sip. You never touched your glass, either."

"Yes, I did," Gail said. "You were just too drunk to notice."

Brayden bolted upright into a sitting position. "Oh, my god! You tried to poison me!"

Aunt Pearl dismissed him with a wave. "Stop being so dramatic, Brayden. You never ended up drinking it, so what does it matter? It's not always about you, you know."

"It matters a lot," Brayden cried. "What if I did drink it? I had so much to drink that I honestly don't remember. And my head is killing me."

"It's just a hangover," Aunt Pearl snapped. "Now, quit interrupting and go back to sleep."

Brayden opened his mouth but thought better of saying anything. He wrapped his arms around his knees and tucked them close to his chest.

"Well, I wasn't too drunk to see what you did, Gail," Earl said. "I drank only a little bit of Amber's eggnog. I watched you the whole night. Watching you watch everyone else, that is. And watching you not take even one sip from your full glass of wine. I knew you were up to something. I just didn't know what it was."

"Liar. I drank plenty." Gail lunged forward in her chair but the ropes restrained her.

"You wanted to kill Merlinda, but you were willing to poison the rest of us in the process." Aunt Pearl's voice shook with rage. "You deserve to die just like Merlinda. I've got half a mind to finish you off right now."

Earl scowled. "I've got some advice for you, Gail. Next time reseal the screw top. Nice guests don't bring already-opened bottles to dinner."

"Okay, my mind's made up," Aunt Pearl said. "You're history, missy!"

"Whoa...hold off there, Pearl." Earl pulled Aunt Pearl close and wrapped his arms around her. He was twice her size, but it wasn't his strength that resonated. It was what he said to her. "Don't do anything you'll regret."

"You're right," Aunt Pearl said grudgingly as she turned to Tyler. "Somebody else can do my dirty work for a change. Sheriff? What are you waiting for?"

<h1 style="text-align:center">CHAPTER 34</h1>

Brayden, Mom, and I stood on the front porch and watched the Shady Creek police van disappear from view. Dominic and Gail were safely in transit to the Shady Creek jail, both charged with Merlinda's murder.

The roads had reopened an hour ago. Our parking lot was full of police vehicles. The Shady Creek coroner and crime scene techs remained on site processing the crime scene for the next few hours at least. Tyler was debriefing them.

What had started as a crime of opportunity had morphed into a crime of passion. I was never good at geometry, but the intersecting love triangles were obvious now in hindsight. I just wished we had figured things out sooner and possibly saved Merlinda from such a tragic end.

One thing still confused me. Merlinda was anything but ordinary. She was a powerful witch, yet she failed to see Dominic's true intentions. I guess love is blind, even for accomplished witches. Even Merlinda had been fooled when her heart was involved.

Aunt Pearl had a faraway look in her eyes. "Merlinda was such a powerful witch. Such raw talent. We'll never see that potential again. Unless…" She turned to me, a hopeful look in her eyes.

"Forget it, Aunt Pearl." I stepped back and shook my head. "You know I don't function well under pressure. Spellcasting won't earn me a living either. I don't want the weight of the witch world on my shoulders like Merlinda had."

Aunt Amber sighed. "Even Merlinda couldn't handle it in the end, now could she? I agree with Cen. So sad. She was such a talented witch but a poor judge of character. You need both to be successful."

Mom nodded in agreement. "That poor girl. I really thought Merlinda had it all. Yet, it seems she really didn't have much at all."

The last few hours had been very telling as we learned of Merlinda's sad existence. It seemed that everyone had taken advantage of her for their own personal gain.

Aunt Amber shook her head. "I can't believe Merlinda's father used her magic to pretend that he had resurrected John Frum and the cargo cult."

Merlinda had merely been a pawn in her father's hands. No wonder she had fled to the relative sanctuary of Pearl's Charm School and Westwick Corners. Maybe she had even delayed her flight home on purpose, hoping to be snowbound.

Dominic had married her for his own benefit too. The very things that gave her power also spelled her demise. Her ultimate cost was her life.

"She made life very profitable for her father," Aunt Pearl added. "Her witchcraft enriched him and made him a big shot on Vanuatu. I'm going to track him down and lock him up in a cargo container. It's time I took a little South Pacific vacation."

As if on cue, Tyler entered the living room. He held up his hand in protest. "Don't interfere, Pearl. I've already been in touch with the Vanuatu police. They're arresting Merlinda's father as we speak. He'll see justice."

"But he's the chief of police," Aunt Pearl protested.

"Not anymore," Tyler said. "He's been fired and replaced by a subordinate who was already conducting a secret investigation of his own. Our findings corroborate his. Merlinda's father won't see freedom anytime soon."

"For what? Murder?" Aunt Amber asked.

"No," Tyler said. "For extortion, fraud, and a few other things."

"He's getting off way too easy," Aunt Pearl protested.

"Don't count on that," Tyler said. "I've been told he's got a lot of enemies that were too afraid to speak up before. Now that he's arrested and fired as police chief, a whole bunch of accusers are coming forward. That probably means more charges."

It turned out that the locals never really bought into the cargo cult scam. Some went along with it because they got free stuff. Others just turned a blind eye and enjoyed the annual celebrations, though many thought Merlinda's father made a farce out of their history and traditions.

Aunt Pearl's eyes twinkled. "I still wouldn't mind a tropical vacation. I sense a business opportunity."

I sighed. "You are not taking over Merlinda's cargo cult, Aunt Pearl. That's better left to history. It certainly won't be well-received by the locals after everything that's happened."

"You can come with me, Cen." Aunt Pearl winked at me. "Consider it an off-campus field trip. Once you see the potential, maybe you'll change your mind. You know, re-enroll in Pearl's Charm School."

"Not a chance." The primary reason Merlinda was such a talented witch was simply because she had put in more hours of spellcraft than anyone else. I had no desire to follow in her footsteps.

Aunt Pearl suddenly grew wistful. "Poor Merlinda wanted nothing more than to use her powers for good, not just to enrich her father. How ironic that he wanted people to think of him as their benefactor rather than the criminal he actually was. He totally took advantage of her. Whatever goods he didn't use himself or for bribes, he sold at a profit. That's how he got rich in the first place."

"I guess he needed to control Merlinda, otherwise his whole plan and power would have gone up in smoke," Aunt Amber said. "Merlinda was the key to his success. Even John Frum couldn't conjure stuff up out of thin air. She was probably relieved when her flight got canceled. She could delay her return."

"She did miss Vanuatu, though," Aunt Pearl said. "I warned her not to go back, but she wouldn't listen. She missed Dominic and said she would just go home for the holidays. I had to act quickly."

"Oh my god, Pearl," Aunt Amber exclaimed. "You really did poison her with that tea. I just knew it!"

"Don't be ridiculous, Amber! How many times do I have to tell you? There was absolutely nothing wrong with my tea. I did not make a mistake, so just give it a rest, okay? That's not how I stopped her from going home. I got her flight canceled instead."

I frowned. "You can't just call up the airline and—wait a minute. Do you mean that you changed the weather? You brought the storm?" I had always thought that conjuring up a blizzard was beyond any witch's ability. "You canceled Christmas for planeloads of people just to keep Merlinda here?"

"You should try it sometime, Cen. All that power over people is mighty intoxicating. You could even outdo Merlinda if you put in a little effort. First, master the snow globe spell, and then…" Aunt Pearl stared wistfully into space.

"I don't want to—oh, never mind." No point arguing. "I still think you should have let Merlinda go home. Trapping her here is kind of obsessive, don't you think?"

"I didn't do it for selfish reasons, Cen. I had to save Merlinda from her father." Aunt Pearl's eyes suddenly grew misty. "I never expected trouble to come here instead. Her father called here day and night, demanding that Merlinda return home. Poor Merlinda felt she had no choice. So I made the choice for her."

Was this really Aunt Pearl? She was sharing her feelings about someone she cared about. I had never known her to do that, ever. "She never told you about the secret wedding?"

Aunt Pearl shook her head. "No. If I had known, I would have stopped it. She confided to me about everything else, so either Dominic's marriage claim was a lie, or else Merlinda was afraid to mention it in case her father found out."

"I guess the truth finally came out," I said. "Poor Merlinda. Too bad fate had plans of its own."

CHAPTER 35

Christmas day dawned quiet and serene. There was no evidence of the wicked snowstorm that had lashed Westwick Corners for most of Christmas Eve. In fact, the weather had warmed substantially.

The storm clouds had lifted to reveal a brilliant blue sky. It was as if last night's unfortunate events had never happened.

Or that they had ended.

I stared out the living room window as I sipped my morning coffee. The early morning sun warmed the snowdrifts, sending rivulets of water down the driveway.

I shivered, despite the roaring fire in the hearth. We were confined to a small corner of the living room as the last few crime scene techs finished gathering evidence. They permeated every corner of the inn, from the dining room and kitchen to Merlinda's room.

Poor Merlinda. Whatever advantages she had in life had ultimately been used against her. She had money and power but was betrayed in the end by love and trust.

"The police won't be too much longer." Tyler had debriefed the

Shady Creek police, and we had all provided statements. There wasn't much more to do since both Dominic and Gail had provided full confessions.

I sat on the sofa and snuggled closer to Tyler. I felt safe and secure with his arms wrapped around me, holding me close. I was grateful for everything I had. I resolved never to take anything for granted. Merlinda's sad fate had given me a fresh perspective on things.

I had a wonderful boyfriend, a loving family, and incredible witchy talents that I could use if I wanted. Even my dull day-to-day existence in Westwick Corners had a certain charm compared to the alternative. I had everything a girl could ask for and then some. What really mattered was what I did with what I had. But making no choice at all was not an option. I had to do something.

My supernatural abilities were mine alone, to be channeled toward whatever I wanted. My talents wouldn't be squandered on mischief or used for material gain. Instead, I would hone my craft so I could use it for philanthropic endeavors to help others.

No doubt Aunt Pearl had an opinion on that. But in the end, it was just that, another person's opinion.

My powers were mine to use or lose. I ultimately controlled them, and it was up to me how I achieved that. But until I took charge of my own destiny, I would be outwitted and out-spelled by more powerful witches like Aunt Pearl. Or worse, fall victim to evil as Merlinda had. If I wanted to be strong, I had to learn my craft and become a stronger witch.

Aunt Pearl.

I scanned the room and was relieved to see her snuggled on the loveseat with Earl. They both snored softly in unison. Earl's hand rested upon Aunt Pearl's green velvet-clad thigh. It was a touching scene. Aunt Pearl normally hid her sentimental side, but here it was on full display.

I briefly considered snapping a picture to embarrass her but decided against it. I didn't want to do anything to discourage her fledgling romance with Earl. He was so good for her. His easy-going nature softened her rough edges. Most of all, he made her happy, though she wouldn't easily admit that.

I was jolted from my thoughts by Aunt Amber. She waved an empty glass in the air. "Who drank all the eggnog?"

"You can't be serious, Amber," Mom said. "It's not even 8 a.m."

"I'm dead serious," Aunt Amber said. "After everything that's happened, I need a drink. I haven't gone to bed yet, so it's not really morning. At least not as far as I'm concerned."

"The eggnog's gone," Mom said. "I gave the last of it to Dominic and Gail. I figured they might as well enjoy some Christmas cheer. It's the last they'll see for a while."

Grandma Vi laughed as she hovered at Mom's side. "I hope it's the last we see of them too."

"Oh, darn." Aunt Amber spun around and headed toward the kitchen. "Wine it is, then."

"Hey, look." Brayden pointed to the hearth where Merlinda's snow globe sat atop the mantel. The globe's flickering light had strengthened into an unwavering sunny yellow glow.

The shimmering Christmas tree lights and the roaring fire warmed the room. But it wasn't just the cozy fire or the company of those I loved. I felt something else, an unfamiliar yet comforting presence. I couldn't put my finger on it, but it was there, nonetheless.

There was something else missing. My Christmas wish remained unfulfilled.

I grabbed Tyler's hand as I stood. "C'mon. I want to show you something."

"You sure? You look like you could use some rest." Tyler's warm brown eyes twinkled as he placed his hand on mine. "I don't think I've ever had such an exciting Christmas Eve. Your family attracts the weirdest people."

I leaned in and kissed him. "It's mostly Aunt Pearl."

"It's all Aunt Pearl," he whispered.

"You sure you want to be involved with my crazy family? You can back out if you want to. You have no idea what you're getting into."

"I know exactly what I'm getting into, Cendrine West." Tyler nodded toward Aunt Pearl, still snoring loudly along with Earl.

It was our first quiet moment since Tyler had arrived for dinner last night, and I wanted to make the most of what little time we had. I wanted my Christmas wish. It was too late for our intimate Christmas dinner but never too late for romance.

I guided Tyler around the Christmas tree so that we were mostly hidden from view. I stood on my tiptoes and fell into his arms for a long leisurely kiss.

That was when I saw it.

At first, I thought it was a Christmas ornament, one I hadn't noticed earlier.

Only it wasn't.

It was a globe, smaller and dimmer than Merlinda's. It rested on the upper branches of the Christmas tree, a foot or so higher than where I had first seen Merlinda's globe.

And it wasn't just any globe. It was my globe. Not the one I had encased Brayden and Gail in earlier but another one. One that I must have created without knowing it during one of my earlier attempts.

It was my Christmas Eve wish right down to the tiniest of details. While Merlinda's globe was a tropical Vanuatu, mine was a snowy Westwick Corners.

I pulled Tyler closer and peered inside the tiny globe. Snow frosted window panes framed the cozy scene inside, a table set for two. It was exactly what I had imagined all along. It wasn't life-sized, but it was my Christmas wish just the same. I had made it come true. I wrapped my arms around Tyler and kissed him.

My globe had been hiding in plain sight all this time, if only I had cared to look.

I broke from Tyler's embrace, eager to share the news. My snow globe was beautiful and strong. And I had done it myself without any help. I especially wanted to prove to Aunt Pearl that my spellcasting was much better than she thought. I thought better of it and pulled Tyler close again.

Tyler smiled. "Some secrets are worth keeping, Cen. It might come in handy sometime."

"You're right." He understood me. He accepted me for who, and what, I was. Even my crazy family. I savored the moment a while longer before we joined the others.

Aunt Pearl stirred on the sofa. She slowly pulled herself away from Earl, careful not to disturb him. "Ruby says I need a break from everything. But I don't know what else to do with myself. That poor girl. I wish I could have saved her."

"I'm really sorry, Aunt Pearl," I said. "I know how much you cared about Merlinda." I had never seen my aunt attached to anyone, much less express it openly. It was a side of her I hadn't known existed.

"It's all right." Aunt Pearl shook her head, but not before a tear rolled down her cheek. "But she was my star student, and I had high hopes for her. Now she's gone just like that." She snapped her fingers.

I turned toward her. "You'll have other students."

"It's just not the same, Cen. Merlinda wasn't like most other students. The only student…"

My momentary bliss turned to irritation. "I'm sure there are other students out there that want to learn. Maybe you need to advertise. You know, promote Pearl's Charm School."

She sniffed. "I don't want just anybody as a student. We have a very rigorous selection process, and I'm certainly not changing that."

"Maybe you could compromise a little. Relax your standards."

It was as if she didn't hear me. "Tell you what. I'll let you come back, as long as you promise to stick to your lessons this time."

"But I'm not ready—"

Aunt Pearl tapped her watch. "Better get a move on. Class starts in one hour." She bolted off the sofa, headed to the front door, and opened it. She stepped outside and then turned back. "I'll get my lesson plan ready. I might regret saying this, but the only student better than Melinda was you, Cendrine. I'm doing this for your own good. One day you'll thank me."

"But I don't want to be a wit—" I realized she had purposely confronted me in front of Tyler, so I couldn't protest. Though Tyler already knew my secret, Aunt Pearl didn't know that he knew. I didn't want her to, either. She had far too much power already.

Tyler smiled and winked. "Maybe you should let Pearl have her way. The whole town's happy when Pearl's happy."

I threw my hands up in the air. I didn't see why I had to be the sacrificial lamb. "I just wish she'd stop trying to run my life."

"Pearl just cares about you, Cen," Grandma Vi said. "She wants you to be the best you can be. Be happy about that."

I was about to answer when something caught my eye.

It was Merlinda's tropical snow globe. It rested in the boughs of the Christmas tree, halfway to the top. It pulsated with energy, lighting up the room like a thousand-watt bulb. In fact, it vibrated with so much energy that I half-expected it to take flight.

"I think Merlinda is trying to tell us something," Grandma Vi said. "She wants you to take her place."

I shook my head firmly.

Aunt Pearl followed my gaze. "You see, Cen? I'm not the only one who thinks that way. In fact, it's my Christmas wish."

"That's a good one, Pearl," Mom agreed. "I'm sure Cen will come around to your way of thinking. Give it time."

"What's your wish, Cen?" Aunt Pearl waved her hand dismissively. "Oh, forget it. If it's something about Sheriff Gates, I don't want to hear it."

Tyler snickered.

"It's a secret." I smiled and thought of my Christmas snow globe hidden in the branches of the Christmas tree.

Aunt Pearl winked at me. "Careful what you wish for, Cen. It just might come true."

How right she was.

* * *

Love Christmas Witch List? Get the next book in the series, *Witching Hour Dead*

www.colleencross.com

AFTERWORD

The Westwick Witches are a product of my imagination, but John Frum and the cargo cult is real. To a certain extent, at least. I've taken liberties in my story, but it's not too far from reality. If you want to read more you can find plenty of historical and modern-day accounts.

John Frum is one of many so-called cargo cults that existed in remote areas in the South Pacific and elsewhere. Frum is the name collectively associated with different seamen who arrived on Tannu, one of the islands in the tiny South Pacific nation of Vanuatu.

Back then, Vanuatu was known collectively as the New Hebrides Islands. Though the islands were remote, they had occasional visitors in the early 20th century, and the islanders were impressed by their modern conveniences and apparent wealth.

However, it was World War II when the cult really took off. 300,000 troops were stationed on the islands, arriving by sea and air. They brought with them all sorts of supplies or "cargo", as the servicemen called their supplies. The troops built Quonset huts, and suddenly, the quiet islands bustled with industry.

The cargo crates included tents, food, medical supplies, and weapons. They also brought the islands first trucks, iceboxes, canned meat, candy, and Coca-Cola too. The quality of life improved immensely for the islanders with all these new mod cons. It was, in a word, magical.

Prior to this happening, the islanders believed in ancient stories and beliefs that had been recorded and retold for generations. It was only natural that some of these fables were combined with stories of the men and cargo that had recently arrived on the islands out of nowhere. From this, the John Frum cargo cult blossomed. Many of the John Frum legends are a mix of ancient beliefs intertwined with modern hopes that the well-equipped visitors brought to Vanuatu.

John Frum may or may not be a corruption of 'John from America', 'John from (wherever)', or maybe something else. Regardless of the name, some form of this cult or pseudo-religion existed well before the Second World War. But the arrival of the troops seemed to be irrefutable proof of ancestral legends. People's beliefs differed: some considered John Frum a religious deity, others considered him a mystical figure, and still others believed him to be a fictional composite of past visitors to the island and better times.

But wars eventually end and so did the troops' time in Vanuatu. In fact, it had ended rather abruptly, just as you would expect a military operation to dismantle once a war ends. The sudden departure meant the end of modern conveniences, since no one else was transporting exotic foods or time-saving household conveniences to the islands.

As the islanders faced their harsh new reality, some believers even created ceremonial landing strips to encourage the visitors to return by air if not by sea. If you've ever lived on a remote island with no mod cons, you'd probably celebrate a made-up fantasy figure too. If strangers arrived out of the blue with all kinds of treasures once, surely it could happen again. It couldn't hurt to cover your bases, right?

Whether it is wishful thinking, true belief, or just an excuse for some fun, many Vanuatuans still celebrate the strange and wonderful conveniences brought by air force planes, naval fleets, and merchant mariners and make predictions for their eventual return. True believers look forward to February 15 of each year as the promised date of return, and even skeptics enjoy the annual parade and celebrations. February 15 is officially observed as "John Frum Day" on Vanuatu.

Kind of makes you think of Christmas Eve and Santa Claus...

I hope you enjoyed *Christmas Witch List* as much as I enjoyed writing it. You can help me to continue to write in the series by providing feedback in an honest review. I read all reviews as they help me to determine the direction of the series, which characters to feature, and whether to continue on with the series or, alternatively, develop a new one.

Thank you so much for reading!

Colleen

ABOUT THE AUTHOR

Mystery and crime thriller author Colleen Cross writes exciting, intelligent thrillers and engrossing mysteries that grip you from the very first page. She took her very own "Exit Strategy" from the corporate world into the book world several years ago to indulge her bookworm wannabe writer self.

Colleen Cross is a retired CPA and CFO who lives with her family on Canada's West Coast. When not writing she loves to run, hike, and explore the coast and mountains with her rescue dog, Jaeger, who reminds her daily that life's too short to not follow your dreams--or a squirrel or two.

Her thriller and mystery books have been translated into multiple languages with more to come. Find them in Dutch, French, German, Italian, Portuguese, Spanish and other languages using search term Colleen Cross

Visit her website at www.colleencross.com and sign up for new release notifications and exclusive subscriber-only offers at http://eepurl.com/bkYx01 or click the QR code below:

Get the latest on Colleen's books here:
www.colleencross.com